MIDNIGHT NECKING

I knelt behind her, glad in a guilty way that her hair was short enough for me to comfortably indulge in nibbling the nape of her neck. Even before my transformation made it a necessity, nape nibbling had been a favorite foreplay activity, among many others, which I now endeavored to put into pleasurable practice.

Quite some time later, she tilted her head back, drawing the white skin taut over the big pulsing vein. We both moaned as I softly cut into her. . . .

THE VAMPIRE FILES

Don't miss Jack Fleming's previous adventures—Book One: *Bloodlist* and Book Two: *Lifeblood*—a thrilling saga of blood and passion as only a vampire could tell it.

The Vampire Files

—— BOOK THREE ——

BLOODCIRCLE

P.N. ELROD

ACE BOOKS, NEW YORK

This book is an Ace original edition,
and has never been previously published.

BLOODCIRCLE

An Ace Book / published by arrangement with
the author

PRINTING HISTORY
Ace edition / October 1990

ISBN: 0-441-06717-4

Ace Books are published by The Berkley Publishing Group,
200 Madison Avenue, New York, New York 10016.
The name "ACE" and the "A" logo
are trademarks belonging to Charter Communications, Inc.

PRINTED IN THE UNITED STATES OF AMERICA

10 9 8 7 6 5 4 3 2

For Mark—
This is as much yours as mine,
And Ben—
The best in the world.
With special thanks to
David Murphy,
who showed us the Dark Side and how to get through it,
and to Paul, Julie, and Christopher Ian,
for letting me borrow your name.

". . . THEN THE DOOR opened and there was this crazy-looking blond guy with a shotgun just standing there, grinning at us. Before we could do anything he swung it up and fired right at Braxton."

"How close were you?"

"To. . . ?"

"To Braxton."

"Pretty close; arm's length, I guess. He knocked against me when he fell. There wasn't much room."

"And to the shotgun?"

"About the same."

"Go on."

"I fell back when he hit against me and cracked my head on a sink—sort of snapped it like this—and that's when things got fuzzy." I paused, expecting him to encourage me again in spite of my faulty memory, but nothing came out. Lieutenant Blair of Homicide, Chicago P.D., had the occupational necessity of a poker face, but I could tell he wasn't swallowing what I was dishing out. He waited and the uniformed cop hunched next to him at the foot of the desk stopped scribbling on his notepad.

I covered the awkward pause by rubbing my face. "Maybe I was dazed or something, but I ran after the blond guy, chased him downstairs and out the building. He was moving too fast and

I was all shaky. I lost him. I went back and told the lobby door-man to call an ambulance. I returned to the studio, saw the crowd in the hall, and began looking for Bobbi—Miss Smythe. When I couldn't find her, I drove to her hotel, but she wasn't there, so I spent the rest of the night looking.''

''You spoke to no one at the hotel?''

''Just Phil, their house detective. He had an envelope for me and I took it.''

''What was it? Who sent it?''

''I don't know, I never bothered to open it I was so busy. I don't know where it is now.''

The cop wrote it all down, trying to keep a straight face.

''I went up to Miss Smythe's rooms. Her friend Marza was there, Marza Chevreaux.''

''Chevreaux,'' Blair repeated, and spelled it out for his man, referring from his own notes.

''She didn't know where Bobbi had gone, either,'' I continued. ''At least that's what she told me.''

''You think she was lying?''

I shrugged. ''Bobbi and I had a fight earlier and Marza took her side. She doesn't like me much and wouldn't tell me anything. I got fed up with her and left.''

''Where did you go after you left the hotel?''

I talked on, telling him of a lengthy search until I found Bobbi in a diner we'd once gone to and how we went out to my car and talked the rest of the night away. When Blair asked the name of the diner, I said I couldn't remember. The cop scribbled it all down until I ran out of things to say, but Blair hadn't run out of questions to ask. We were in his office, which was better than an interrogation room, but at the end of my story he looked ready to change my status from witness to suspect.

''When did you next see the blond man?''

''I didn't,'' I lied.

''Why did he shoot Braxton?''

''I don't know.''

''Why was Braxton after you?''

"I don't know."

"You told the hotel detective, Phil Patterson, something else. You told him Braxton was a con man. Why?"

"Mostly so Phil would be sure to keep a watch out for him and keep him from bothering Miss Smythe. I thought that if Phil thought the guy was a troublemaker he'd be extra careful." At least that was the truth, and Blair seemed to know it. "Braxton was crazy, too. Who knows why he was after me? I never got the chance to find out."

He paused with his questions and I wondered if I'd tipped things too far. He looked at the cop and with a subtle head-and-eyebrow movement told him to leave, then settled in to stare at me. I stared back, attempting a poker face and failing. I'm a lousy liar.

Blair was a handsome man, a little past forty, with gray temples trimming his dark wavy hair, and full, dark brows setting off his olive skin. Too well dressed to be a cop, he was either on the take or had some income other than his salary. His upper lip tightened. He was smiling, but not quite ready to show his teeth yet.

"Okay," he said easily and with vast confidence. My back hairs went up. "This is off the record. You can talk, now."

I looked baffled, it wasn't hard.

"All I want is the truth," he said reasonably.

"I've been telling—"

"Bits and pieces of it, Mr. Fleming, but I want to hear it all. For instance, tell me why you waited so long to come in."

"I came when I saw the story in the papers."

"Where had Miss Smythe gone?"

"To some diner, I forget—"

"Why did she leave the studio?"

"She wanted to avoid trouble."

"What trouble?"

"*This* kind of trouble. She used to sing at the Nightcrawler

Club, got a bellyful of the gang there, and quit to do radio work.''

''Yes. She quit right after someone put a lead slug into her boss. It's interesting to me how death seems to follow that young woman around.''

''You think she was involved with that mess?'' It was meant to rattle me, but I was on to that one.

He just smiled.

''Then think something else,'' I said, leaning back in my chair. ''Her boss gets scragged and she quits, there's no surprise to that. A couple of the other girls did the same thing. You can check.''

''I have. She was Morelli's girl as well as his employee. . . . And now she's your girl.''

It wasn't a question, so it didn't need an answer.

''Did you tell her to leave the studio?'' he asked.

''No, I—''

''Why were you at the studio? You said you'd had a fight with her.''

''It wasn't much of a fight. I went there to make up with her.''

''And Braxton followed you . . .''

We walked through the whole thing again and I told the truth about what happened, but left out the motivations. Blair didn't like it, but he wasn't quite ready to get tough yet. He kept shifting around with his questions, trying to trip me somewhere.

''And then you went looking for her instead of—''

It was time to show a little anger. ''Yeah, so I didn't stay put—I wasn't thinking straight. I see a man cut in two practically under my nose, maybe come that close to it myself, and I'm supposed to hang around to make a statement?''

''No, but you did go chasing after an armed man and disappeared for two days.''

''Stop dancing and tell me what you're getting at.''

He continued as though I hadn't spoken. ''In the meantime, the man turns up in his car near his home, peppered with wooden pellets—"

"Huh?"

"—as though from a shotgun wound. Instead of rock salt or lead, someone loaded the cartridge with small wooden beads. Can you explain that?"

I shook my head.

"The man was half-dead from numerous other injuries and in a mental state one might charitably describe as shock. How did he get that way?"

"I don't know. Ask him, why don't you?" I was on firm ground here. That blond bastard would never put together two coherent words ever again. I'd made very sure of it.

Blair shifted the subject again. "Who was the woman in his house?"

"What woman?"

He pulled out a photo and tossed it to me. A sincere pang of nausea flashed through me as I looked at the starkly lit image on the paper. The harsh blacks and whites had their full-color match in my memory of the scene. I tossed it back onto the desk. "God, what happened to her?"

"Someone took her head off—with a shotgun; maybe the same weapon that killed Braxton."

"The blond guy must have done it."

Then who did it for the blond guy? his expression seemed to ask me. "Why was this woman wearing Miss Smythe's red dress?" he asked aloud.

"What?"

"Miss Smythe wore a bright red dress to the broadcast; many people remember it. Somehow it ends up on this corpse. Why?"

"There must be a mix-up. Bobbi still had that dress when I found her. It must have come from the same store."

His eyes were ice cold, like chips of polished onyx. "Come along with me." He got to his feet and walked smoothly around the desk.

"Where?"

He didn't answer but opened his door and motioned for me to go out first. We walked down a green-painted hall and went into another, smaller room. It had a scarred table, three utilitarian chairs, and one bright overhead light, its bulb protected by a metal grille. On the table was a sawed-off shotgun, tagged and still bearing traces of fingerprint dust.

"Recognize it?"

"Looks like it could be the one the crazy used on Braxton, except when I saw it the barrels seemed about that big." I held my hands a foot apart to indicate the size.

"And what about this?" From the back of a chair he picked up a dark bundle that unrolled into the shape of a coat. The front lapels were ragged and an uneven hole the size of my fist decorated the middle of its back where the blast had exited. The edges were stiff with crusted blood.

"Looks like mine," I admitted, not liking this turn of evidence.

"We found it at Miss Smythe's hotel."

"I keep some clothes there so she can have them cleaned for me; she insists on it. I changed to another coat—I couldn't hunt for her looking like a scarecrow."

"Are you sure it's yours? Put it on."

I shot him a disgusted look, but decided to go through the farce.

"It fits you."

"All right, so it's mine."

He was busy examining the hole in the back. "Looks like the shot must have gone right through you."

"I had the coat draped over my arm at the time. Maybe it got between Braxton and the gun at just the right moment."

He shook his head. "The physical evidence we have doesn't support that, Fleming."

"What does it matter? You have the killer."

"Take that off and have a seat. We're going to discuss how it matters."

"You charging me with anything?"

"That depends on your willingness to cooperate. . . ."

He'd moved to one side so I could get to a chair, and stopped dead, his dark eyes flicking from something behind me to my face and back again, his jaw sagging. I could hear his heart thumping, though his breathing seemed to have stopped. Turning around I saw a mirror set in the wall behind me; a one-way job so someone next door could keep an eye on things. From Blair's new angle he could see the whole interrogation room reflected in it, and as far as the mirror was concerned, he was alone.

"Something wrong?" I asked, changing coats. I tossed the old one onto the table. As it left my hand its reflection appeared in the mirror, having jumped out of nowhere. That was interesting.

Blair had lost his voice as well as his calm confidence and hadn't moved a muscle except for his widening eyes. They kept twitching from me to the mirror. They settled on me one last time and he took a quick breath, reaching instinctively for the gun holstered in the small of his back. A shoulder harness would have been faster, but it would have also ruined the lines of his suit.

I shook my head, maintaining a steady eye contact. "Don't do that."

His movement ceased. Completely.

I gulped. It wasn't easy because my mouth was bone dry. After a moment I was calm enough to work up enough spit to talk. "Let's go back to your office," I suggested. "You lead the way."

We went. I sat down; he remained standing until I told him to sit as well. He slipped automatically behind his desk, his face blank and waiting.

"About what happened in the other room . . . you hear me, Blair?"

"Yes." His voice was flat, distant.

"I identified the gun and coat to your satisfaction. You didn't notice any problem with the mirror, understand?"

"Yes."

"Then we came back here. My guess is the woman in the photo was murdered by the blond man. Her red dress probably came from the same shop as Miss Smythe's. That sounds right, doesn't it?"

"Yes."

"In fact, you think I've been very cooperative. You have got Braxton's killer, after all."

"Yes."

"That's good. You can relax now and do your business as usual—we're good friends." I had other people to protect than myself, so my conscience wasn't kicking too hard.

My hold on him melted away, but not my influence. He got on his phone and rattled off some instructions for someone to type up my statement and bring it in for signing. While he did this, I looked away and studied some framed items on the wall. A few were documents, the rest were pictures of Blair shaking hands with city-hall types. He liked to have his photo taken; he took a good one. On his desk was a studio portrait of a smiling and very pretty girl.

"You married?" I asked by way of conversation. I wanted to pass the intervening time on neutral subjects.

He looked where I gestured—normal again without my control—and literally brightened when he saw the girl's face. "Not yet."

"Soon, huh?"

"Not soon enough for me." His smile was sincere now, not the cold one calculated to put a suspect on edge. "Her name is Margaret."

"She's a real dish. You're a lucky guy."

We made small talk about his fiancée until the other cop returned with a typed version of my statement. I read it over and signed.

"Sorry it took so long," said Blair. The cop gave him an odd look.

"That's all right, I know how it is." I made to go, and Blair escorted me out of the building and even shook my hand. He liked me. Inside, I cringed a little at the power I had over the man and was glad to turn my back on him and walk away.

Parked down the road just under a streetlight was a gleaming black Nash. A man with a beaky nose and a lot of bone in his face emerged from it as I approached. He was tall and thin and almost as well dressed as Blair, but in a quieter style.

"How did it go?" asked Escott.

I sighed out my relief from habit rather than a need for air, but it felt good, so I took another lungful. "As Gordy would say, 'no problem.' "

"They believed you?"

"They didn't have much of a choice. I just sometimes wish I were a better liar."

"The way things are going, you're sure to have other opportunities to practice. Shall we go on to the hospital and see what else we can patch together?"

"Visiting hours will be over by now."

"We'll get in."

Escott was sure of himself because he seemed to know almost everyone in Chicago. I didn't question him. We entered the hospital without a hitch and even the most territorial and authoritative nurses gave way before him. He knew how to turn on the charm when he felt inclined, and we left the last of the guardians of good health giggling at her station.

"How did you do that?" I asked.

"I'm not sure, but if it works, I shan't try to analyze it. Perhaps it's to do with my accent."

"You mean if I learn to talk like Ronald Colman—"

"I do *not* speak like Ronald Colman."

"Sure you do, like just now with Tugboat Annie back there."

"Don't be absurd."

Escott's English accent was more clipped and precise and less leisurely than Colman's, but I argued that the effect was the same. Getting him to bristle was a novel experience for me. The debate kept us entertained until we turned the last corner and saw the cop in a chair next to a numbered door. He regarded us with interest and stood as we approached.

"I'm Dr. Lang," Escott told him. "Dr. Reade asked me to look in on the patient for him."

"Ain't it kinda late?"

"Yes, it is," he said wearily, "and this is hopefully my last call for the night."

"I'll have to see your pass."

"Show him my pass," he said to me.

I got the man's full attention and flipped out my old press card. "It's all in order, officer," I told him.

He didn't even blink. "Okay, you can go in."

"Thank you." Escott did so—all but grinning at the situation—with me right behind him.

It was a private room, furnished in cold steel and white enamel, with one small light glowing in a corner opposite the single high bed. The slumbering occupant was obscured by rumpled sheets and a mass of bandaging around the top of his head. His breathing was slow and deep, our entrance hadn't roused him.

Escott hung back by the door, ready to deal with the cop in case he walked in.

"I don't want to do this," I whispered.

He understood but shook his head, his humor gone. "But you have to do something. So far they're blaming the head wound for his story, but you can't let him continue to talk, especially if some of the more irresponsible papers get hold of it. You dare not take that chance."

"Yeah." Damn.

He was right. We'd been all over it before and couldn't think of any other alternatives. Indirectly, this would help protect Bobbi and Escott as well as myself, so that should have made it easier, but I'd still have to be very careful.

I cat-footed to the bedside and looked down at the sleeping boy. He was Matheus Webber, chubby young friend to the late James Braxton, and he'd come very close to death himself that night at the radio station. Both had been hunting for me with the mistaken idea that I was a menace to society. They'd assumed my normally friendly disposition to be false and had set out to kill me with the best of intentions and a lot of misplaced zeal. Their knowledge of my true nature and needs was limited, and they'd placed a superstitious reliance on crosses and silver bullets to control and destroy me. They'd been annoying, but nothing I couldn't handle until Braxton got in the way of another, much more effective killer.

Matheus was now telling the story of their hunt for the vampire to anyone who'd listen, but so far his parents, the medical staff, and the cops thought he was crazy from the concussion he'd suffered. But if he kept talking, someone else just might begin to believe the story in the same way as Blair. Once he'd seen a hint of the truth of things, it had all fallen into place for him, necessitating my direct influence on his mind. There were too many mirrors in the world for me to take any more risks.

I folded back the sheet and blanket to get a better look at the kid. What I saw would have decided me if I hadn't already made up my mind. Escott craned his neck for a look to see what made me stop and frown. He frowned as well, but refrained from giving me an "I told you so" look. The patient wore a big silver cross around his neck with a couple of bulbs of whole garlic threaded together on a string. He had at least gotten someone to humor him. It was a step in the wrong direction as far as I was concerned.

The boy's eyes opened slightly. He didn't know me at first, mumbled a sleepy question, and rolled onto his back. I put a hand on his shoulder and said his name. He shot fully awake—but never got the chance to scream.

* * *

Escott was driving; his big Nash was one of the central pleasures of his life. For the first time in several harrowing nights he seemed relaxed enough to look content. His eyes were filmed over and far away, as though he were listening to music, but as always, his brain was clicking.

"You look like you've consumed a sour apple," he observed. "Was it really so bad?"

"What solves a problem for me could make one for him."

"In what way?"

"You know what I mean. I'm off the hook now, but what if he comes out with psychological measles later because of my monkeying around?"

"You've read Freud, then?"

"Never had the time so I don't know about that. I do know I shouldn't be doing what I'm doing. . . . It could be bad for the kid."

Just like Blair, Matheus's face had gone blank. It was easy, so damned easy. I could put anything into his mind I wanted; twist it up like an old rag for the garbage and leave it for other people to clean away. It happened before: by accident with my murderer and on purpose with Braxton's murderer. Both men were insane and not likely to recover. Matheus didn't deserve that.

"I don't think you've done him harm," he continued. "You suppressed no memories."

Which would have been too noticeable by everyone. If the kid woke up with no recollection about his trip to Chicago with Braxton, someone might get too curious. People tended to prefer the answers they already had to dealing with new questions, so I played on that.

Instead, he'd wake up and realize that Braxton had been a crazy old man using and misleading an impressionable kid. There'd be some unavoidable embarrassment for Matheus, but he was in the real world now, safe from the paranoid nightmares of a crackpot.

Go to sleep, kid. You'll feel a lot better about things in the morning.

"He'll soon put it all behind him once he's home," Escott added.

After all, there are no such things as vampires.

He hauled the wheel around and swung us close to the curb. "Our train leaves in two hours; I'd like to be there early to make sure your trunk is properly seen to."

"Hour and a half from now?"

He glanced at his watch to get the exact time. "I'll be back by then."

I almost asked him where he was going, but it was unnecessary. He was planning to simply drive. His eyes were already darting around the dark and nearly empty streets with anticipation.

"Please say hello to Miss Smythe for me."

"Sure."

The door shut, he shifted gears, and glided off. I crossed the walk to the hotel entrance and went in. Phil Patterson was at his usual spot, leaning against the pillar near the front desk. His crony, the night clerk, was making typewriter noises in the office and for the moment the lobby was dead. Phil nodded a neutral greeting in my direction.

" 'Lo, Fleming. Straighten things with the cops?"

"Yeah, we got everything all worked out."

"Blair tough on you?"

"Couldn't say, I don't know how tough he can get. We didn't have any problems."

He nodded, but there were a lot of thoughts and questions behind it. "Too bad about that little guy, Braxton. They ever figure why he got bumped off?"

"The killer's going to the nuthouse soon, maybe the head quacks can figure it out. Till then . . ." I shrugged.

"Guess we'll never know," he agreed, watching me hard.

"Yeah, too bad." My voice was a little tight and forced. He noticed, but let it pass. I owed him a favor, a big one for getting the muzzle of a gun pointed elsewhere besides my chest when it went off. I'd have survived the experience, but explaining why to a room full of people would not have been easy. Phil decided not to call in the favor just yet.

The kid in the elevator knew to take me to four without being told and hardly looked up from his magazine. He was deep into Walter's 110th Shadow novel, *Jibaro Death*. I'd have to remember to pick up a copy of my own to read on the train.

. . . the power to cloud men's minds . . .

I smiled and shook the thought out fast. That gimmick was strictly for the radio show and certain supernatural creatures of the night—not the book character. The main difference between me and the Lamont Cranston on the air was that he had fewer scruples about using his talent.

Bobbi's door was locked and no one answered my tap. The hall was clear so I vanished and slipped right through, which was a bad move. Marza Chevreaux stepped into sight from the kitchen just as I solidified. She was fiddling with the clasp of her necklace and walked like a movie holdup victim, elbows pointed up and head tilted down. She was a fraction too late to actually see my indiscretion, but nearly jumped out of her garters when she looked up and saw me standing in the entryway.

"Hello, Marza, I knocked—"

"I heard, but I was busy." She gave me a long, unpleasant stare, the kind usually reserved for roaches when they go spinning down the toilet. "That door was locked," she stated.

I glanced back and tried my best smile of baby innocence on her. "I had no trouble getting in."

She swiveled her head toward the closed door of Bobbi's bedroom and back to me again. "No, I suppose you didn't," she said in a nasty tone, and went to a table to dig through her handbag. She stuck a thin brown cigar in her mouth and fired a match.

For five seconds I thought unkind thoughts, but didn't voice them. That sort of indulgence is always wasted on people like Marza. "What put the bug up your butt tonight?"

Just like a dragon, she pushed blue smoke from her nose and snapped the match out as though it were a whip. "It's what you are."

"Which is . . . ?"

"A two-timing bastard who beds one girl while chasing after another," she said casually.

That was a relief. At least she wouldn't be coming after me with a hammer and stake. "You can hardly call it two-timing, since I haven't seen the other girl in five years."

"So you've told Bobbi."

"So I'm telling you. It's the truth."

"She believes you, I don't."

"Is that all that's bothering you?"

"You're leaving town to look for this other one. What happens to Bobbi when you find her?"

"That is none of your business."

"It is if Bobbi gets hurt."

"I don't plan to hurt her."

"Like you didn't plan for that goon to kidnap her?"

"Did Bobbi explain to you that Escott and I are doing this to make sure it doesn't happen again?"

"And do the cops know you're leaving town?" she asked sweetly.

"The less they know, the better it is for Bobbi."

"Don't worry, I'll keep my mouth shut for her sake—"

"That'll be nice."

"—but the best thing you can do for her is to go and stay gone. We don't know who you are. You hang around with Slick's old mob, you've got money but no job, the cops want you for murder—"

"I cleared that up tonight."

"You got Gordy to pay someone off, you mean."

"Lady, you're crazy. And I wouldn't be so hard on Gordy; if it weren't for him, we'd never have found the goon—"

She knew she was losing and grabbed up her bag, unlocked the door, and walked out, not bothering to slam it. I shut it, very carefully and very quietly. The woman was enough to make a preacher cuss, and at the moment I was feeling anything but Godly minded.

"Marza? Is that Jack?" Bobbi's voice floated out from her bedroom and had an instant brightening effect on me. I forgot all about Marza as Bobbi came out and rushed over to hug me.

"You doin' okay?" I asked the top of her head. Her silky platinum hair had been crudely chopped off by the goon, but she'd been to the beauty parlor for repairs and it looked fine now.

"God, I thought you'd never get here," she mumbled into my chest.

"We had a busy night."

"What kept you so long?" she demanded, pretending to sound nettled. "Was it the cops or that Webber kid?"

"Both, but neither should be any trouble now. How about telling me why Marza's in such a cheerful mood? She looked like a snake bit her, only the snake died."

"She's gone?"

"Once she saw me, she couldn't get out fast enough. Have I sprouted horns or something?"

"No, but it is because of you."

"So I figured. What's the problem?"

"She blames you for what happened to me."

"And not unreasonably. What'd you tell her?"

"Only what you said to say, that your old girlfriend's sister wanted something from you and had used me to get it."

"She want to know what it was?"

"Of course, but I said I didn't know and you weren't talking. It's hard on her, not getting the truth."

"I think it'd be a lot harder on us both if she did."

"Maybe she'd prefer knowing what you are to thinking you're in the mobs."

"Uh-uh. She's not as understanding as you. You sure that's all there is—she just thinks I'm in with Gordy's bunch?"

"No, I've talked with Madison, he said she was pretty

upset that night. There was some kind of scene and you got her drunk.''

"She was ready to take my face off so I made her drink something to calm down. It was purely in self-defense. I'm just glad Madison came in when he did, she needed a shoulder to cry on and mine wasn't available for various reasons.''

"But you saw her like that, all vulnerable.''

"Nothing wrong there.''

"She thinks so. She's usually so in control of herself and now she's embarrassed because for once she wasn't.''

"That's hardly a good reason to hate my guts.''

"It is for her.''

"Then she needs a doctor.''

"It's just artistic temperament.''

"I'd call it something else. What are we talking about her for, anyway? I came to see how you were doing.''

"It takes my mind off things, Jack,'' she said, wilting a little against me. "I never said I didn't have nightmares.''

"I wish I could help, baby.''

"You do.'' She wrapped her arms more tightly around me. We ended up on the sofa, hanging on to each other as though it were the end of the world. Some of the feeling leaked out of her eyes, but she took my handkerchief and dabbed it away. "What'd you say?'' she asked.

"I'm sorry.''

"What?''

"I'm sorry that all this happened. Marza was right. If it hadn't been for me, you—''

"Jack.'' She pushed away to look me in the eye.

"Yeah?'' I wasn't so sure I could look back.

"Shut the hell up and give me a kiss.''

I double-checked. She'd meant it, so I stopped stammering and followed through. She let me know in no uncertain terms that everything was all right between us.

"Y'know,'' she said, coming up for air, "Marza thinks I should stop seeing you.''

"What do you think?"

"I think she's an idiot butting in where she don't belong."

Then we picked up on things again, and the flat got very quiet except for Bobbi's breathing and the whisper of our hands.

"You staying the night?" she murmured.

"I want to, but I've got that train to catch. Charles is coming by later to pick me up."

"You sure he needs you along?"

"No, but he seems to think so. He says he wants my help, and it is my problem—what are you doing?"

"You're smart, you work it out." She pushed the lapels back until my coat was off, loosened my tie, and undid a few buttons at the neck.

"You sure you're up to this? I know you've been through the wringer."

"Let's find out."

She was wearing her favorite style of lounging pajamas, the satin ones with the high Oriental collar. The top opened up with a minimum of fuss and, as usual, she'd neglected to put on underwear. She turned her back to me, slid free, and pulled my hands around to her breasts.

Her skin was all that a woman's skin should be, her strong body all any man could wish to know and possess. I knelt behind her, glad in a guilty way that her hair was short enough now for me to comfortably indulge in nibbling the nape of her neck. Even before my transformation made it a necessity, neck nibbling had been a favorite foreplay activity, among many others, which I now endeavored to put into pleasurable practice.

Quite some time later, she tilted her head back, drawing the white skin taut over the big pulsing vein. We both moaned as I softly cut into her.

THE HOLLOW-EYED image in the dark glass was a sinister version of Escott's sharp face. I settled in opposite him. He glanced at me, then contemplated my apparently empty chair reflected in the window between us. Beyond it the last lights of Chicago sped or dawdled past, depending on their distance from the train. We had the smoking car to ourselves and Escott puffed on a final pipe while the porter was busy elsewhere making up his compartment for the night.

"Something funny?" I asked when the corner of his mouth curled briefly. For him, it was the equivalent of a broad grin.

He gestured at the window with the pipe stem. "I was only recalling the night I first noticed this about you at the train station and what a shock it had been."

"Yeah, what were you doing there, anyway?"

"At the station? Using the train, of course. I had returned from the completion of some minor out-of-town case. It was quite a shock to look up and see something that wasn't there." His eyes traveled to the window again.

"Most people would have figured they were seeing things and shrugged it off."

"Most people see many things, but few ever draw sensible conclusions from them."

"And right away you concluded I was a vampire? Not too sensible."

"Hardly," he agreed. "I'll admit I did initially think your lack of a reflection was from some trick angle of the glass, but eliminated that option after a few moments of observation. The conclusion that you were a vampire was the result of an improbable line of reasoning. Improbable, but obviously not impossible. I've read my share of lurid literature."

I looked at the empty spot in the glass for a long time, cautiously touching the feeling of eeriness mirrors now inspired in me. After nearly a month in my new life I was still not used to the way they ignored me. It was a constant and irritating reminder of my isolation from the rest of humanity. On those occasions when I was feeling particularly low, it was as if I no longer existed at all.

"And after all that reading you still wanted to risk meeting me?"

He rested his head on the back of his chair and closed his eyes. "There were many small indications that it was less of a risk than you would think. Trifles, really, but important trifles. A person's posture and movements reveal his soul far more clearly than his words, and once one has studied this alphabet of expression, the thoughts flashing through a man's mind are as easy to read as a child's primer."

"How'd you figure all this?"

"My theatrical background: in order to imitate life, one must first study it. When I first noticed you, your movements and expression suggested a deep preoccupation with some problem, but an energetic willingness to face it."

"Maybe I was worried about finding a victim to drain."

"Perhaps, but after witnessing your purposeful walk to the stockyards, I concluded you had no need to subsist exclusively on human blood."

"Unless I was hunting up some handy worker there."

"Why go there when more convenient meals were strolling the crowded streets? If it were very difficult to isolate a pedestrian for some nefarious purpose, the crime rate for mugging would be strangely low."

"I hadn't thought of it that way."

"After you emerged from the yards, your posture had not changed. You still had a problem and it was not hunger. At that point I knew I wanted to arrange to meet you and to find out more, so I intruded myself—"

"I wouldn't call it an intrusion now. You just wanted to get my attention."

"You are most forgiving on that point."

"Why not? I got my earth back and you got your questions answered. Everything turned out all right."

"True." A lazy puff of blue smoke rolled slowly to the ceiling and his eyes opened a crack, studying me. After another puff, he said, "I was wondering if everything was all right now."

It was pretty vague and at the same time a pretty personal question, at least for him. "What d'ya mean?"

"I'm inquiring about your physical and mental state after that stairwell incident. Are you all right?"

A simple yes would have been the easy and obvious answer, but he wasn't one to ask casual questions, so I thought things over until I concluded I felt fine. It was crazy, too, considering I'd been staked in the heart and left to die by inches in my own blood.

Without passion I remembered the silent, paralyzing agony in the blackness, the near-insanity, and the final icy cold creeping up to claim me forever. Ultimately, in my mind, I saw my would-be killer as I'd left him: his face blank, his eyes staring pinpoints, and his mouth hanging slack. I'd left him as he had left me, except no one would come by to save him, now or ever. No one could.

It might be a popular conception in some circles that vampires are selfish creatures of pure appetite, that we can only take. In the brief time since my violent rebirth I'd learned that we are able to give of ourselves. I believe it's a way of venting off all the negative stuff that gets stored up in the memory, leaving only the memory, but not the destructive emotions. I'd freely given mine away to a man who deserved them. He was forever lost in my nightmare and would never wake from it again. I had no regrets.

"I'm fine," I said at last, and meant it. "Been reading my posture or something?"

"I did that on our way to the station."

"Yeah? So what trifles did you observe and conclude from them?"

He kept his eyes on the darkened city slipping past our window. His tone was kindly and amused. "My dear fellow, there are certain things a gentleman just does not discuss and still expect to be considered a gentleman."

I went a little red in the face. "What about you? Are you okay?"

He dismissed his own feelings with a decisive wave of his pipe. It was what he didn't say that filled my head now. He'd read the papers and talked to the cops and doctors. By now he knew all about what I'd done to the man. Apparently he had no regrets, either.

We'd booked a double, but Escott had it all to himself. My place of rest was elsewhere on the train, and I remained in the smoking car long after he'd gone off to bed. It was lonely; no die-hard insomniacs were aboard, and the staff had better things to do than keep me company. I got busy reading a fresh copy of *Jibaro Death* that I'd bought at the station newsstand. It kept me busy over the next few hours, though it was poor occupation when compared to my recent time with Bobbi. Sometimes I'd drift out of the plot entirely and catch myself looking at nothing in particular, no doubt with a sappy smile on my face.

Toward dawn I moved on to the baggage car and slipped inside without getting caught. Buried deep among the tons of suitcases, crates, and other luggage was my own traveling bedroom—a lightproof and very sturdy trunk. It was large enough to hold some extra clothes, a sack filled with my home earth, and me, though it was less than comfortable to someone with my long bones. Standing vertically as it was now, I'd have to rest my rump on the sack with my knees crowding up by my ears. During the day the awkwardness of the position hardly mattered; as long as the earth was next to my body I slept the sleep of the dead.

No joke.

Outside the car I could sense the searing, blinding sun start to roll above the horizon line. I quickly folded away my magazine, sieved into the trunk, and let the rocking motion of the train ease me safely out of the world for another day.

I'd been alive once, in the normal sense of the word. In that time, I'd met a woman and fallen in love. All the clichés I'd ever read about the subject had turned out to be absolutely correct. Floating—not walking—around in a gauzy pink haze of giddy happiness, I could charitably understand how the power of love had changed the course of human history. I felt a kinship for other courting couples and pity for those who were still searching.

Maybe Maureen's nature set us apart and made us feel unique from all the others who'd ever been in love, but I didn't see it at the time and still don't. Love is love and I'd have felt the same about Maureen no matter what. You see, Maureen Dumont was a vampire.

Of course, she wasn't the kind of white-faced, blood-obsessed zombie found on the screen at the Bijou down the street; she wasn't the freckled girl next door, either. She was rare and special and so was our relationship, and we were smart enough to know it. We took steps then in the hope of making our love last beyond my own short life span. The one thing the books and movies do get right is our method of reproduction; it takes a vampire to make a vampire—only there's no guarantee it will work. You can get into bed, make love and exchange all the blood you want, but the change won't necessarily happen or there'd be a lot more of us around. Maybe it's like a rare disease and nearly everyone is immune to it.

In my case it was a success. One traumatic night I woke up dead—only Maureen wasn't there to see it happen. Five years ago she'd packed a few things together and vanished, leaving me a cryptic note with a promise to return when she felt safe again. She never returned.

I'd waited and then searched for her. Not knowing if she'd been caught by the people she'd feared or if she'd grown tired of me and wanted an easy way to say good-bye, the bewildering pain was still inside me, fresh and harsh after all the years in between.

I'd finally decided to try to leave it behind, desperate enough to quit my job with a New York paper in the middle of the Depression to attempt another start on life in Chicago. My efforts caught the attention of the people who had also been hunting her. One of them had been her younger sister Gaylen, who had been as murderous as Maureen had been gentle.

Escott and I had managed to survive that encounter, and now we were outward bound to pick up where he'd left off on his trail after Maureen. He was a professional, and damned smart, and I trusted him enough to take care of things on his own, but he insisted I come along this time. Between us was an informal agreement to work together, so I came, willing to render whatever help he thought I could offer, but doubting our chances of success.

We arrived in New York during the day, so I was completely out of things while Escott took care of the business of getting us routed to our hotel. His plan was to check in, then hop a train up to Kingsburg. Maureen had had Gaylen confined to an expensive asylum there, and Escott wanted to talk with her doctors again. He must have had a hectic time before he took off; when I came to at sunset my shoulders and spine were all twisted and aching. A sloppy wooziness sloshed between my ears and I felt oddly heavy all over.

Outside the trunk, a door opened slowly and closed

abruptly and Escott muttered a pithy exclamation. My confined world lurched, tilted, and whumped solidly onto the floor. He clicked the key in the lock and pushed the lid up.

"Mm?" I said, still dizzy from being on my head.

"Terribly sorry, old man. I didn't have time to see you to your room. The train schedule was just too close. I distinctly told the fellow how I wanted your trunk placed and he deigned not to listen."

"Welcome to New York," I said philosophically and winced at the blinding dregs of a new dusk burning through the thin curtains. The sun was officially down, but more than enough light lingered in the sky to be painful. I fumbled for my dark glasses and found they'd slipped from their pocket and were burrowing into my ribs. One earpiece was bent, but they were still serviceable, and I slipped them on with a sigh of relief. Sometimes I really hate waking up.

"How are you?" he asked, walking to the open window and considerately pulling down the shade. A stale breeze made it flap a bit. It was the familiar used air of a big city, but some thirty degrees cooler than the stuff we'd left behind in Chicago.

I rubbed the sore place on my head and a few grains of dirt from my bag of soil trickled to the floor. "Gritty."

He liked puns, but only when he was making them. "Facilities are just over there if you wish to refresh yourself."

I did and got untangled from my mixed-up belongings and staggered into the bathroom to splash cold water on my face. "How was Kingsburg?"

He dropped into a fat chair, stretched his long legs out straight, and looked smug. "I have the address of Gaylen's next of kin—"

"Next of kin?"

"—to be notified in the event of an emergency."

"It's not Maureen, is it?" I'd read that from his attitude.

"No, it is not Maureen, but some other woman named Edith Sedlock."

I'd never heard of her and said as much. "Where is she? Have you checked on her?"

"She lives here in Manhattan, and I've not had time to look her up."

It flashed through my mind that Edith could be Maureen. "Let's get going, then."

He held up a cautionary hand. "You'd create a better impression if you had a quick wash and brush-up."

"Damn." But he was right; I looked rumpled and felt the same. Spending twelve hours packed in a trunk does that to a person.

He checked his watch. "There's a café off the lobby just left of the elevator. I'll wait for you there. Thirty minutes?"

"Fifteen."

He'd just finished his sandwich and I gave him no time to linger over the coffee. Playing native guide for a change, I led the way to the nearest subway station, taking the fastest route to the address we wanted.

"How did you manage to get it?" I spoke just loud enough for him to hear over the background noise of the train. "I thought doctors were first cousins to clams."

"By talking a great deal."

"The Ronald Colman bit, huh?"

"Hardly. I merely told them the truth . . . some of it, anyway."

"How much is some?"

"That I was hired by an interested third party to search for Gaylen's missing 'daughter,' Maureen. I had only to show them my credentials and a stunning letter of reference."

"Letter of—" Then the dawn came. "You mean you're still packing all that stuff from the blackmail list?"

"I haven't had time to return it yet and it seemed a waste not to use it in a good cause."

"But how could it be used?" I wasn't accusatory, just curious about his mechanics. As far as I knew, the stuff in his safekeeping consisted of nothing but embarrassing photos and indiscreet letters and documents.

"There *are* ways. I simply hinted around that my client was very prominent, but wished to remain anonymous. When pressed, I reluctantly revealed an important name on a miraculously appropriate letter, one of a most interesting series. It was child's play to keep my thumb over the name of the original addressee."

"Jeez, don't you take the cake. What did you learn from them about this Edith Sedlock?"

"They believe her to be Gaylen's other daughter."

"Other—Maureen's got another sister?"

"Possibly."

"She'd have to be a younger woman if the Kingsburg doctors thought her to be Gaylen's daughter. Then she could be—"

"Like you, yes, but I am not inclined to think so."

"Yeah? Why?"

"Because she was able to answer the phone during the day when they called to tell her of Gaylen's escape."

"Maybe she was rooming with a human friend."

"There's that," he conceded. "She instructed them to keep her informed on the situation, and that's all they were able to tell me about her."

"Would they phone her about you?"

"I'm sure they already have. Anyone else searching for Gaylen would certainly be of interest to the next of kin."

"Did Maureen leave any other address for them?"

"Her own—that is, the one you originally gave to me. All the bills for Gaylen's care were sent there and promptly paid via Western Union. Did Maureen always pay in cash?"

"As far as I know, when she did buy anything. We didn't exactly spend a lot of time shopping."

"Yes, and I know you hardly keep banker's hours. I did find out something quite interesting: the date of Gaylen's escape coincides exactly to the date you found Maureen's note."

That was no real surprise and made a lot of sense. "I wish she could have found some other way of handling things than by running."

"Perhaps she once tried."

"What d'ya mean?"

"In the same situation, what would you have done to neutralize Gaylen as a threat?"

"Same as I did to Matheus, I guess."

"But no matter what the provocation, she might have been most reluctant to do so with her own sister. You weren't happy with the idea yourself."

"Yeah . . ."

"Or perhaps Gaylen's will might have been strong enough for her to resist such an imposed influence. The woman was utterly obsessed with getting her own way and quite mentally unbalanced, considering the lengths she went to to finally achieve her goal."

"Tell me about it," I grumbled, and thought about Bobbi with a pang of guilt over what she'd been put through. "I hope to God we can clear this up now."

"As do I," he agreed, and left me alone with my thoughts until our stop came up.

We emerged in the east fifties and walked a couple of blocks south to Forty-eighth and a promising line of brownstones. It was a respectable working-class neighborhood with a few shops along the street, a drugstore on one corner, and a quiet little tavern at the other. We found the right number and went up.

Edith Sedlock lived in the back corner flat on the third floor, and her door remained firmly locked as she asked our business.

"My name is Jack Fleming," I called through the plain panel of wood. "I'm a friend of Maureen Dumont—"

"Maureen?"

"Yes, we've just come from Kingsburg—"

A key clicked and the door opened exactly four inches. Two dark brown eyes glared at us suspiciously. She had matching brown hair, bobbed short, and was nearer thirty than forty. Aside from the giveaway of her age, she had a strong and fast heartbeat. She was definitely not a vampire.

"What's this about?" she demanded.

"May we come in and tell you, Miss Sedlock?" Escott asked politely, his hat in hand. I took the hint and grabbed mine off.

Still doubtful, she stepped back, swinging the door wide and leaving it open after we walked in. She looked us over carefully, frowning, but apparently we weren't too threatening. She gestured us to a small lumpy sofa.

It was a simple one-room flat, and the place was littered with too much furniture, clothes, books, magazines, loose papers, and used dishes. A radio sang to itself on a table next to a tiny stove and sink. She turned it off and dragged a wicker chair from the table and sat facing us, her knees and ankles pinched tightly together and her hands yanking the hemline of her dark dress down as far as it could go.

"Our apologies for intruding on you, Miss Sedlock," Escott began.

She interrupted. "I've been expecting to hear from you. The sanatorium called me. They said you'd been asking after Gaylen Dumont. Are you Mr. Escott?"

"I am."

"May I see your identification?"

He solemnly opened his wallet, she peered at it, then at me. In turn, I peeled out my old press card for her inspection. She sniffed at both of them, vaguely dissatisfied. With her, it was probably a chronic condition.

"It's out of date," she said to me. She looked as if she wanted to find fault with Escott's but couldn't think of anything.

I put my card away.

"You're very observant," Escott commented neutrally.

"I have to be, I'm a teacher."

"No doubt you are quite good at your job." He was turning on the charm again, but keeping it to a low level so as not to scare her off. From the pallid pink spots that appeared and vanished from her cheeks it seemed to be working, too.

"How did the sanatorium come to give you my name?" she asked.

It was Escott's show, so I gave him the nod. He explained about our search for Maureen and that he had at least located her mother as having been a patient at Kingsburg. Since Gaylen Dumont was no longer in residence and since he had excellent references, the administrator there had every confidence in Escott's professional discretion. The doctor in charge had no qualms in giving out the name listed as Gaylen's next of kin.

"Yes, I'm sure *he's* got every confidence in you, Mr. Escott, but his lapse in releasing such information is nonetheless deplorable; hardly what I would have expected from a doctor."

"I agree, but the circumstances of this situation are most unusual. Believe me, we have no wish to impose upon you any longer than necessary." He was being utterly sincere. No doubt he found her personality just as grating as I did, but was better at hiding it.

Her frown softened a little, but not by much. "Well, at least they did call and tell me about your visit, though I think they should have first asked my permission before giving out my name to just anyone walking in."

"Quite so," he agreed, all sympathy.

She sighed, affecting a slightly world-weary exasperation at life in general and said, "All right, now that you're here, what do you want?"

"As I said, we are trying to trace Maureen Dumont. We thought—"

"First of all, I am *not* related to the Dumonts, and second, I have no idea where Maureen is. I haven't heard from her in years."

"How many years? And how did your name come to be—"

"July or August, 1931," she stated. "It was a little over five years ago. We were neighbors at the same apartment building back then and lived next door to each other. She asked if I'd mind taking deliveries and phone messages for her during the day if I happened to be at home. She worked at night, she said, and hated having her sleep disturbed. She said she had to follow a very strict schedule because of her health and get so many hours of sleep or become ill. She was quite serious about it, as I never saw her during the day, but her other hours were very irregular. She wasn't one of *those* women, at least, or I wouldn't have had anything to do with her. I don't know what she did, but she was a quiet neighbor, and that counts for a lot with me."

"What about the last time you heard from her?" I asked.

"I'm coming to that. When the crash came, it upset everything for me, and I had to move. I kept the same phone number, though, and so we kept the same message arrangement as before. I expect she got someone else to take her packages. As for the sanatorium, she'd asked if she could put my name down along with her own for next of kin. The idea was that if anything should happen to her mother and they called during the day, I could pass the call on to Maureen in the evening. It seemed a reasonable precaution, so I didn't mind. The only call for her was when her mother escaped. I immediately tried to call Maureen; it seemed enough of an emergency to justify waking her up, but I couldn't get hold of her till evening."

Escott nodded, soaking up every syllable. "Can you tell us her exact words?"

"No, not after all this time, but she was very upset. I thought she'd go right to pieces then and there. I asked if I could help in some way, but she said she had to think first and hung up. About three hours later, she called and left a number where she could be reached if they had any more news of her mother. She sounded a lot calmer by then, and made a point of saying I was not to give the number out to anyone. The old lady was quite dangerous and violent despite her years, and Maureen wanted to take no chances on being found by her. It's a terrible shame that she was so terrified of her own parent, but that being the situation, I promised.''

"Would you object to giving the number to us?"

"What makes you think I still have it, Mr. Escott?" Her lips thinned a bit into a kind of smile.

"You have me there, Miss Sedlock," he admitted, responding with a warm one of his own.

She must have been trying to flirt with him. She liked his reaction. She went to a small phone table, picked up a flat address book, and brought it back to her chair. She flipped through the pages until she came to the Ds, and read off a number penciled in next to the neat ink lettering listing Maureen's name and former address. Escott carefully copied it down.

"That's a Long Island exchange," I said. "What was she doing out there? Did she say?"

"No, I don't think so, presumably she was getting help. It was a very short call, we didn't want to tie up my line in case the asylum had to get through to me."

"So she didn't give this number to the asylum?"

"Obviously not," she sniffed, "or she wouldn't have bothered giving it to me. Besides, Mr. Escott would have gotten it from them during his visit there."

Escott acknowledged her deduction and returned her out-of-practice smile with another of his own. She responded with a near-wiggle. "Did the asylum ever call you?"

"The next day, but nothing had changed."

"Did you try the Long Island number?"

"Of course I did. Some man answered, I asked for Maureen, but his manner was very off-putting, as though he were surprised. He asked how I'd gotten his number and I told him, then he wanted to know who I was, but I only gave him my first name and asked for Maureen again. He said she had left and wanted to know who *I* was, but I said Maureen would know and hung up."

"You have a very clear recollection of that conversation," said Escott.

"Yes, I do, don't I?" She considered it a moment. "I think it was because he was so insistent. It made me uneasy. I never called back."

"Uneasy?"

"Silly, isn't it? After all, he was only a voice on the phone; an ordinary voice, except for his accent."

"What kind of accent?"

"Almost like yours, but not quite."

"An English accent?"

"Not quite."

"Perhaps from another region there?"

"No . . . I think that it was more American than English, but I couldn't place it now. I just noticed at the time that it was unusual."

"And you heard nothing more from Miss Dumont?"

"No, and the asylum called only one more time. They'd notified the local police, of course, but they wanted to talk to Maureen, and by then I didn't know what had happened to her. I expect they were waiting for her to call them."

"Didn't you think it odd?"

"I most certainly did, but what could I do about it? I went by her apartment to see her, but she was gone. The landlord said he thought she'd moved out. She'd left behind most of her clothes and books and other things, so it seemed likely she might return. The landlord wasn't too concerned. She'd paid her rent, but he was planning to put her things into storage in the basement if she wasn't back by the end of the month."

"Did he have any theories?"

"No."

"And you didn't contact the police?"

"I thought about it, but didn't see how they could help. Besides, from what I heard, someone else was looking for her, and he'd have done all that. The landlord said that Maureen's boyfriend was always pestering him for news of her return."

I had trouble finding my voice, but just managed. "And you never thought to contact him?"

"Yes, I did, but for all I knew he might have been the unpleasant man on the phone." She sniffed again. "If she wanted to cut things off with him, that was her business, not mine."

I had no choice: I could walk out or strangle her.

I walked out.

Escott came down a few minutes later and found me hunched against a street lamp trying to light up a smoke. My hands were shaking so much I couldn't even fire the damned match. I finally threw it and the cigarette into the gutter.

"That stupid, idiotic bitch!"

Escott listened patiently while I raved along similar and much more obscene lines for some time until I wound down into coherency again. We walked for several blocks and the movement and damp night air helped to cool down my frustration.

"I am in total agreement with you," he said in a mild tone when it was over. "She might have saved you a lot of anguish had she spoken to you then, but we've yet to see if her information is of any value."

"Then let's find out."

We went back to our hotel and Escott started out with a phone call. First he checked with the operator to make sure the number was still in service, and then he got an address and name to go with it.

"Emily Francher?" I said, echoing his inquiry. "No, I've never heard of her."

"You don't sound too certain."

"I'm not. I don't think I've met her personally, but maybe I saw her name in the paper or heard it on the radio. . . ."

"Perhaps it was an advertisement," he suggested, his eye falling on the newspaper he'd bought in the lobby stand when we'd returned. He tilted his head, considering his own thought, and noisily attacked the paper, tearing open the pages in a sudden fit of energy. "There." His long finger stabbed at a name.

I stared at it awhile. "Naw, it couldn't be, not the shipping line Franchers, that's just too big. Maureen never mentioned she knew anyone like that."

"You've also stated she never talked about her past," he pointed out.

"Well, yeah . . ."

"It may only prove to be a coincidence of names, as it was rather easy to trace the number, but first thing tomorrow I shall check it out thoroughly."

"Tomorrow?"

"Indeed. The sources I intend to exploit are all closed by now—"

"But we could rent a car and drive out there."

"I plan to do just that, but only after I find out all I can about this Emily Francher first—and about the man who answered the phone."

"The one who made little Edith uneasy?"

"The same. Granted, the woman is certainly a touch paranoid as far as men are concerned—"

"You can say that again."

"—but for her, the form it takes is that of bossiness and a general hostility."

"I get you. Her normal reaction should have been to tell him off when he got nosy?"

"That or ignore him. But I'm getting ahead of my research. It is Miss Emily Francher I shall concentrate on in the morning."

I idly flipped the pages of the paper. "Then that's it for tonight as far as the investigation goes, huh?"

"Regrettably, it would appear so."

Disadvantages abound with my physical condition, and spending the day locked up in a lightproof trunk is the one that irks me the most. I miss out on a lot of life, and once awake and free, I try to make up for the lost time.

"The last thing I feel like doing now is to sit around in this fancy box the rest of the evening," I told him. "What about you?"

"I hadn't really thought of it. I was going to unpack and perhaps listen to the *March of Time*, but if you feel restless—"

"Yeah, I'm restless, but it's no fun trying to cure it alone. I want to find some entertainment."

"It does sound somewhat more distracting." He glanced at his watch. "A pity, but it's past curtain time by now."

"A play?" I rustled the amusement page around, folding it to the outside. "This is New York, Charles, they've got more than plays going on. Here we go, *Swingtime* is playing at Radio City and a new place just opened called *The Paradise*—"

"Well . . ."

"Here, this is the one, *Folies d'Amour*, three shows a night and dinner thrown in with the jokes and dancing girls."

He looked a bit shocked as he scanned the details of their ad. "Good heavens. Have you noticed the two-fifty cover charge?"

"You get what you pay for. Besides, this is my idea and my treat. You know as well as I do that I don't spend any money on food, so how 'bout it? I know I could do with some high kicking."

He chuckled suddenly. "It sounds most educational."

We took a cab and got there in time for the last half of the second show and stayed on for the third. Escott enjoyed his late supper and didn't seem too put out when he had to imbibe drinks enough for two in order to cover for me with the waiter. They had little visible effect on him other than a slight glazing of the eyes, but then he looked the same way when driving his Nash.

Outwardly he seemed more interested in the mechanics of the production than the show itself, and his conversation was limited to comments on the efficiency of the crew involved.

It was hard to tell, but I eventually concluded that he was indeed enjoying himself. The glazing disappeared from his eyes at intervals, usually when the girls in their spangled costumes were strutting their stuff to the brassy music.

The wee hours were upon us when the place finally closed down. The air was a humid mixture of exhaust, oil, and hot tires . . . and something else, very faint and distant. In response, there was a familiar and insistent stirring in my belly and throat. I lifted my head to catch the scent again, but it was gone.

"Like the show?" I asked between my efforts to whistle up a cab.

Escott put a lot of thought to the question before coming up with an answer. "Very much. Next time it shall be my turn. I hope that you will then have no objections to seeing a play?"

"None at all. I wanted to see a show like this just to get the taste of Edith Sedlock out of my mind."

"It was an excellent idea," he said, enunciating carefully. "I must admit I do prefer a stage production of any kind to a film, though I've nothing against film as a medium for entertainment."

"Your acting background has nothing to do with it, huh?"

"It has everything to do with it, my dear fellow."

"Why'd you leave it for this business?"

"Why, indeed?" he asked the general air, looking just a shade wistful.

"I mean it, Charles. From what I've seen, you're a born actor. Why'd you switch to being a private inves—private agent?"

"Because taking up acting as a profession is a good way to starve to death. The company I was in folded for lack of funds—that is to say, the manager stranded us. I made it my business to find him. It was my first case."

"Did you find him?"

"Yes, after a time. I even recovered the money he'd stolen and divided it with the rest of the company. This, of course, after I'd indulged myself and thumped the miscreant a few times so he wouldn't object to things. It was interesting work, so I decided to go into it.''

"Thumping managers?''

"Finding things; doing things for others.'' He waved his hand vaguely.

"Wouldn't acting be safer, though? I mean, since you took up with me, it's been—''

He laughed a little. "You've obviously never tried staging the battle of Bosworth Field in a barn full of drunken lumberjacks. When King Richard started calling for a horse, they were more than happy to oblige him with one. No, I much prefer to do what I'm doing now, there is a certain exhilaration to this kind of business that I never found on the stage.'' He took a deep breath, held it, and let it out slowly.

Perhaps he'd realized he was talking about himself and his attitudes rather than about things he'd done, which was his usual run of conversation. On certain levels, he was a very private man. I pretended not to notice and waved unsuccessfully at another occupied cab.

"I think it is long past my bedtime,'' he concluded after a long moment. "If I begin quoting Shakespeare to no good purpose, please bring it to my attention and I shall cease immediately.''

A cab finally pulled up and I got the door for him and shut it. He gave me a questioning look.

"I've still got a lot of night left to me. Thought I'd take a walk in the park.''

He nodded, perhaps guessing the real purpose of my walk. "Right. Then I'll see you tomorrow evening.''

The cab grumbled away into the night, its exhaust swirling around my ankles. When it had grown small and its lights had merged with dozens of others, I abruptly turned in the opposite direction. I walked quickly, my head raised to catch that tantalizing scent once more.

IT WAS NINE long blocks along Seventh to Central Park. I covered it quickly, my mind focused upon what lay ahead. This sort of careless behavior can lead to a mugging or worse, but no one bothered me, not even to bum a cigarette.

There are stockyards of a kind in New York, but nothing that could be fairly compared to the huge landmark in Chicago. Cattle are shipped in by rail each day to be slaughtered, many of them to support the large Jewish population and their kosher requirements. Maureen had taken me there once, but I had no need to travel so far tonight in search of livestock; not as long as Central Park had pony rides and horse-drawn carriages.

I knew more or less where the animals were kept, and in due time my nose led me to some stables. It was the same smell that had caught my attention outside the club, carried to me by some freak of the faint wind. Maybe it was an unpleasant odor to some, to me it meant food. I slipped inside and quietly got acquainted with its half dozen four-legged tenants, picking out a healthy-looking gelding with a calm eye.

Having spent some formative years on a farm, I knew how to talk to horses; I almost didn't have to soothe him to quiescence. I did so anyway, just to be on the safe side. The animal stood placidly while I opened a vein in his leg and slowly drank my fill.

The hollow, near-cramp in my stomach vanished. The almost-ache in my throat eased to nothing. Most of the time, the symptoms of my hunger were negligible and could be ignored if I were busy, but I was careful never to let it go too far. It wasn't that I'd lose control and be tempted to drag someone into an alley to feed off them, I just disliked the physical discomfort that resulted from waiting too long.

It was my first taste of horse's blood and I liked it better than the stuff I'd taken from cattle. There *was* a difference to it; not so much in the subtleties of flavor and texture, but in the surroundings. This was a neat, straw-cushioned stable, not a soggy, stinking pen. The animal was clean and the hair on his hide short. When you have to get to your food by using your own teeth, that counts for a lot.

Afterward, he politely accepted being patted down in lieu of a more material show of thanks. Next time around I'd remember to bring an apple or some sugar cubes. It seemed only fair.

When I crawled out of my trunk the next evening I found Escott at his ease on his bed, showing no ill effects from his sedate debauch, and up to his neck in the papers.

"Good evening," he said cheerfully, hardly looking up.

"How'd it go today?" I asked, stretching.

"The *London Times* has finally dropped its pro-Hitler policy in favor of the Russians, who seem to be the lesser of two evils at the moment. It was that speech he made last Sunday at Nuremberg that did the trick."

"I *meant* with the—"

"Oh, yes, sorry." He folded the paper away. "Emily Francher, daughter to the late Roger and Violet Francher—"

"The shipping-line Franchers?" I interrupted.

"The same."

"I'll be damned."

He continued. "Emily was one of the better-dowered debutantes in 1913, and was sole heiress to the estate when her mother died in 1931."

The coincidence of the date wasn't lost on me. "When, in 1931?"

"I've a lot to tell you, but I'd rather tell it on the drive out."

"Out to—"

"Yes, the Francher house on Long Island. I've a map and hired some transportation, having assumed you would want to interview Miss Francher personally about that phone call. The sooner you are ready . . ."

"Okay, okay, I'm moving!"

I did all the usual stuff, and shaved with my eyes closed so I wouldn't have to look at the gaping emptiness in the mirror. It takes a little practice and a good memory so as not to miss any spots, but I was in a hurry and nicked myself this time. Vampires bleed red like anyone else, it just doesn't last as long from a metal cut.

"If they made safety razors out of wood, you'd need stitches," said Escott from the other room.

"How the hell did you know I'd cut myself?"

"By the timbre, volume, and quality of your language. Far be it from me to laugh at another's pain, but you are most entertaining when you choose to express yourself."

"Next time I'll charge admission," I grumbled.

Our rented Ford eventually got us free of the congestion of Manhattan and Queens, but it seemed to take forever. Escott had to concentrate on driving, while I kept us on course with the map, so we didn't talk much. Once past the worst of it and safely rolling on State 25A, I was ready to hear more about our destination.

"You said this Emily Francher was quite the dish in 1913?"

"I said she was well dowered. I don't know what she looks like. The money and her mother helped her to land a socially acceptable husband. In this case, he was an impoverished gentleman with a title from my own sceptered homeland.''

"So maybe his was the nearly English accent Edith Sedlock heard on the phone.''

"I think not. The marriage was at her mother's forceful instigation and short-lived. The blissful couple parted company a month after the ceremony, the bride taking up residence in London and the groom in the north to be near the races.''

"Gambler?''

"Gentleman jockey. He broke his neck in a steeplechase later that same year and much to the disgust of his mother-in-law, the family title passed on to an obscure and fertile cousin with a surplus of sons. Daughter Emily was ordered back to New York and resumed the use of her maiden name.''

"Where'd you dig all that up?''

"It was in the papers. The society gossips had a fine time then, but it was only a foretaste of what was to come. Roger Francher died in 1915 and wife Violet took over the shipping business and proved herself most capable. She also set about looking for a suitable replacement for her inconveniently deceased son-in-law. By this time, young Emily had suffered what we would now call a nervous breakdown and was sent off to 'rest' with relatives in Newport, who reported her every utterance to the mother. Efforts to locate another title were thwarted by the war, but in 1920 the lady managed to befriend a French marquis and whisked him across the Atlantic to meet Emily.''

"Did Emily have anything to say about this?''

"If she did, her mother was quite uninterested.''

"And the Newport relatives?''

"Dependent upon Violet's generosity for their support. Another wedding date was set, but it all fell through when the groom was arrested. It seems he was not a marquis or even French, but an American with three other wives.''

"Three?''

"And a number of children. They tried to suppress the scandal, but were unsuccessful with some of the less discriminating papers. Officially, the wedding was postponed for an indefinite period while he returned to France to 'settle his business interests.' In reality, I'd say he was lucky to only have to face the French courts and his several families and not Mrs. Francher. He might have gotten away with having a fourth wife had the lady been less publicity minded and not issued his picture to every society editor in the Western Hemisphere.''

"*His* picture? What about Emily?''

He shrugged. "Perhaps her mother didn't think her an important enough participant in the proceedings. From what I could glean between the lines, the bride was once again less than enthusiastic over things.''

"I guess it was just as well. What happened to her?''

"By then she had come into her own inheritance from her father's will and bought a house on Long Island. I think it was an attempt to make a life for herself away from her mother.''

"Better late than never.''

"Violet still tried to interest her in another titled marriage—she was a very single-minded woman—but was distracted from any serious efforts by her own involvement with the shipping line. When the crash came, she lost most of the business, and rather than doing her daughter a favor and leaping from her office window, she turned things over to the board of directors, officially retired, and moved in with Emily.''

"Nice lady.''

"Their past separation did seem to do the girl some good. Having her own money, she built a house for her mother on the same grounds as her own estate and invited her to take possession. The invitation was firmly declined, so Emily moved instead. It was just as well for her, because her former home burned to the ground in April of 1931 and Violet Francher along with it.''

I thought awhile on that one. ''You think Emily might have killed her mother?''

''That is always a possibility. The most vicious and unforgiving crimes often occur as a result of frustrations building up within families. Emily might certainly have had sufficient cause over the years to resent the woman enough to do murder. The investigation ruled it to be an accidental death.''

''What do you think?''

''Not having had access to all the facts leading up to those results, I think nothing at all.''

''Why was there an investigation, then?''

''It was the standard thing to do in such a case. A sum of insurance money was involved, though the amount was trifling compared to Emily's assets.''

''Rich people can be greedy, that's how some of them get to be rich. How did Emily keep her assets through the crash?''

''She took to heart the maxim of Anita Loos's heroine that 'diamonds are a girl's best friend' and put her trust in safe-deposit boxes rather than her bank account.''

''Smart girl.''

''Since the fire, she's taken up the life of a virtual hermit, albeit a hermit in extremely comfortable circumstances. She still supports some of her poorer Newport relations, but never visits them.''

''You learn anything about who answered the phone?''

He shook his head.

''What about that breakdown? Is she still loony?''

''I have no information on her current mental state. Her past experience might have been connected to the decease of her father. The story at the time consisted of a few bald statements about resting her nerves—''

''Which is the same as going nuts. I had an idea she might have been sent to Kingsburg instead of Newport for her rest cure. It'd give her a logical connection to Maureen.''

"That's a good idea, but the dates involved are too disparate. There was also considerable documentation in the social columns pertaining to Emily's presence in Newport."

"Only if you believe everything you read."

"How much truth is there?"

It was a straight inquiry, not a rhetorical question. "In general, or—"

"In the papers. I should be interested in hearing from one who has been on the inside of things."

I didn't have to think long or hard on that one. "It depends on the reporter, his editor, and the kind of rag they work for. If you want to boost circulation—and who doesn't?—the truth can be victim of enough exaggeration to sell papers, but not so much that it courts a lawsuit. It also depends on the kind of information picked up. The best journalist in the world can make a goof if he's given false or incomplete information, or if he misunderstands what he gets. Unless editorializing is the main angle, we try to give people the truth. When you've got a deadline breathing down your neck every few hours you don't have time to make things up."

Since he'd exhausted his information about Emily Francher, the conversation shifted to journalism, with me doing most of the talking and Escott soaking it up as he drove. We were now passing through a different world from Manhattan; less than ten miles from the Queensborough Bridge were working farms and their villages. Minute museums housed in buildings dating from the American Revolution advertised displays of relics from that period.

Off to the left side of the road we got an occasional glimpse of Long Island Sound, smooth and sullen in the moonrise. I wore my dark glasses against the glare.

I checked the name of the last village against our map and a fast five minutes later I told him to hang a left. We began a tour through the exclusive country of the very rich. We were closer to the sound than ever, but couldn't see it for the trees that were packed so close to the road they formed a tunnel.

Traffic was light, which meant nothing passed us coming or going unless you counted the rabbits.

"This is it," I said.

On the left was a fifty-yard stretch of brick wall, broken by a fancy gate with the name FRANCHER arching over it in white painted ironwork. Inside stood a very solid brick gatehouse, showing some muted lights. A white gravel drive twisted out of sight into the trees beyond. Escott tapped the brake, parked the nose of the Ford next to the gate, and hit the horn a few times.

A light came on outside the gatehouse and eventually a short man emerged and squinted at us. He wore an old hickory shirt, hastily buttoned, and gray work pants, stained at the knees. The lower half of his face was sunburned.

"What do you want to bet he's the gardener?" I asked, but Escott wasn't taking.

The man came within a few feet of the gate, trying to peer past our headlights.

"Who's there?" he called.

Escott introduced himself, said he was a detective and that he needed to speak with Miss Francher about an investigation he was conducting.

"Huh?"

I gave him a sympathetic look. He cut the motor, got out, and went up to talk with the man. It took a lot of time and much waving of his Chicago credentials. The man dithered a lot and said "I don't know" a lot, and Escott got nowhere fast.

Another figure appeared from the house; a thin, sinewy woman with her graying hair braided for sleep. She wore the standard black of a maid's uniform, minus the white collar, cuffs and apron, and had shoved her bare feet into her thick work shoes.

"What is this?" she demanded both of Escott and the man. By his behavior in her presence, it was likely he was her browbeaten husband.

Out of his depth, he made a partial start on an explanation, was shushed by the woman, then Escott had a turn. He repeated his introduction with his hat off and I noted he was emphasizing his English accent. This time it didn't wash and she suggested he come back tomorrow afternoon. Miss Francher was not in the habit of receiving uninvited callers after dark.

Escott wasn't put off. He mentioned again the vital importance of his case and asked that a message be relayed to Miss Francher. He would abide by her decision. He wrote something in his notebook and tore out the page. Frowning, the woman accepted it between thumb and forefinger as though it were especially dirty laundry. She snapped something at the man and stalked back to the gatehouse with him in tow.

Escott came over to my side of the car and leaned an arm on the roof and a foot on the running board.

"What'd you write?" I asked.

"A request to talk with her about Maureen Dumont. It tips our hand, but at this point it would seem to be unavoidable."

"What if Emily tells us to get lost?"

"Then we apparently drive away. You can quietly return later."

"And tiptoe up on her for a private interview?"

"You've acquired some experience at breaking and entering by now, and I know you have very little trouble persuading people to talk once you've gotten their attention."

"Yeah, but I'd rather go through regular channels, if you don't mind. I hate scaring people."

"With that attitude, you could give vampirism a bad name."

After a few minutes I caught the sound of a motor coming our way. The gardener was driving a rattle-trap old truck with shovels, rakes, and similar tools sticking out the back. They clattered and rolled around as the thing growled over the uneven gravel surface. He hopped out and opened the gate for us. The woman emerged from the house again to glare at

Escott. She obviously wasn't happy, having been denied official sanction to tell us to go to Halifax.

She pointed at the gardener. "Follow him, he'll take you to the main house."

Escott wasted no time starting the Ford up again and driving us through the fancy iron bars. The woman closed and locked them, and we followed the little truck up the drive at a stunning seven miles an hour.

The grounds were semi-wild; the grass was uncut, but the trees were trimmed and no fallen branches or brush cluttered the spaces between them. The drive curved, slanted slightly uphill, crested, and sloped down again to a large, unnaturally flat section of ground. An almost perfect square was outlined by scarred trees and stunted shrubs.

Escott nodded at it. "I can safely say that that must be where the burned house once stood."

Past the plateau marking the house, the land continued its long slope to the sound.

"Maybe Violet hadn't wanted to move because of the view," I said. "What caused the fire? Do you know?"

"They traced it to some worn-away insulation on a table lamp. It shorted out and set fire to a rug and then went on to the rest of the house. The mother was asleep upstairs and probably died of smoke inhalation without ever waking. The body was still in bed when they found it."

"Except for the plants, you wouldn't know anything had ever been there. That must have been some cleanup job."

"I expect the present mistress of the estate may have found the ruins somewhat depressing."

Another turn, more trees, and then a glimpse of buildings made of white stone with cream-colored trim. I made out a two-storied garage separated by the gravel drive from a much larger structure. The trees parted. Maybe it was modest when compared to some of the other houses in the neighborhood; it couldn't have had more than fifteen or twenty bedrooms at the most. Lights were showing on both floors and at the porte cochère–style front entrance. The truck stopped beneath it and so did we. The gardener escorted us to the open double doors, handing us over to a younger woman uniformed as a maid. She smiled a neutral welcome and gestured us inside.

The entry hall was only a little smaller than Grand Central and furnished with slick Italian marble and Impressionist paintings, which caught Escott's immediate attention. Beautifully framed, labeled and perfectly lit, I didn't have to ask if they were genuine; they wouldn't dare not be.

At the far end of the hall was a massive staircase, also of marble. The wall on the upper landing held a series of huge canvases that marched off out of sight on either side. They depicted fantasy scenes of people playing in gardens. I didn't know enough about art to put a date on them, but the white powdered wigs and wide skirts made me think of Versailles before someone invented the guillotine.

The maid had thoughtfully given us a moment to stare and get used to things, then led us to the right and to a smaller room. The marble floor was replaced by an intricate pattern of oak broken up by Oriental rugs. The fireplace was in use, and soft shadows from the antique furnishings danced in the far corners and were lost against the dark background of the paneled walls.

Under a single lit lamp by the fire, a woman on the young side of middle age sat in a massive red leather chair. She had crisp, shiny black hair, cut short and dressed in perfect waves along her skull. Her skin was sallow and just starting to bag along the jaw and stretch at the neck. She wore a long red velvet dress that clashed with the chair leather and enough diamonds to set the country's economy straight again. Hundreds of them hung from her neck and arms, catching the glow from the fire and throwing out glints and sparks like the Fourth of July. In full sunlight she'd have been blinding.

She watched our approach with a mixture of wariness and interest.

"Mr. Escott?" Her voice echoed her expression.

"Miss Francher?" Escott bowed very slightly and introduced me as his associate.

"Have you an affliction of the eyes, Mr. Fleming?"

"No, ma'am," I said apologetically, and folded away my dark glasses.

"That's better. You may sit down. Coffee or tea?" she asked without enthusiasm, and we declined the offer with thanks. Social necessity out of the way, she dismissed the maid and inquired about our business.

"As I mentioned in my note, I am working on a disappearance case," Escott began. "We're looking for a Miss Maureen Dumont, who vanished in the late summer of 1931. We know she made a telephone call to an acquaintance and gave your phone number to them—"

"You mean she called from this house?"

"We can assume she did. She said she could be reached at this number." Escott read it off from his notebook.

"That is my number, but I don't know anyone named Dumont," she stated flatly.

"She might have used a different name," I said. I described Maureen to her. She listened, but ultimately shook her head.

"I can't help you, I'm sorry. May I ask why you wish to find her?"

It was an effort to talk. "She was . . . she was special to me. Her disappearance was unexpected and unusual. I've been looking for her since then. This is the first solid clue I've had in five years . . . there must be something you can remember about that summer."

Emily Francher again shook her head, her expression clouding as she swallowed and looked away. "My mother died that year. Things were very difficult for me and I was on medication for much of the time. My memories of that period are most painful and I've done my best to try to forget them."

"I can understand that, but—"

She held up one hand. "I have led and continue to pursue a solitary life. I have very few visitors. I am certain that if this young woman had come to my house specifically to see me, I would have known about it."

"Even back then?"

"Most certainly back then. The only visitors I received were members of my family and my lawyer to settle up any legal matters. They were all people I knew—this Maureen Dumont was not with them. Now, either a mistake has been made on your part with the telephone number, or one of my staff is involved, in which case my secretary will help you. Jonathan?"

Two high-backed chairs were placed in the far corner of the room, turned away from the center of things. Until now, neither Escott nor I had known one of them was occupied. The man she'd called to stood easily and came forward to look us over.

He was too handsome to be real, that's how he struck me at first glance. His dark hair was perfectly combed, his features just uneven enough to be interesting and arresting. He didn't have to smile for me to know his teeth would match the rest of him for a correct turnout. He wore a sober, well-cut suit with a subtle stripe that picked up the color of his blue eyes. He was tall, with a good spread of shoulder and not much hip, just the type to have to beat women off with a club. Some twenty years younger than his employer, I could guess that he was secretary in name only. If rich men felt entitled to have mistresses, I supposed rich women could have their gigolos as well. It was no skin off my nose.

"Jonathan, this is Mr. Escott and Mr. Fleming. Would you please see to them?"

He nodded acknowledgment. "Certainly, Miss Francher. Please come this way, gentlemen."

Escott caught it at the same time and telegraphed it to me by a brief change in his eyes—an accent, almost English, but not quite. He swallowed back any objections to our summary dismissal by the lady of the house, bowed slightly again, and thanked her for her time. She waved a benevolent, if somewhat vague hand, and picked up a book from the table next to her chair.

The secretary led us on a short hike to the second floor and ushered us into a cross between an office and a sitting room. It had more paintings on display, and Escott stopped and fairly gaped at a dim, heavily framed portrait of a man with a lumpy nose. Even my uneducated eye recognized it as a Rembrandt. It had to be genuine, nothing less would have been tolerated in such a house.

Opposite the door were some tall French windows softened by pale curtains. They opened onto a veranda that ran the length of the back of the house and overlooked a large, well-lit swimming pool. Though it was a cool night, someone was splashing around below. I wandered over to the rail for a better look and saw a slim blond girl cutting through the water like a seal, doing laps.

"That is Miss Francher's cousin, Laura," said the secretary, drawing my attention back into the room. "She's very fond of swimming," he added unnecessarily.

He politely settled us on a long couch and eased himself lazily into a padded banker's chair before a rolltop desk. The top was shut and a whisper of dust clouded its brass handles.

On closer look, and in better light, he was still a remarkably handsome man. His dark hair and expressive brows accentuated his pale complexion, and slender blue veins were visible under the fine-textured skin of his long hands. He suddenly seemed out of place in his fashionable suit and modern surroundings. He should have been on a movie screen swinging a sword around and romancing Merle Oberon or Greta Garbo.

"How long have you worked here?" I asked.

"Several years." He looked me over carefully in turn, holding on to a faint smile and not the least discouraged that it wasn't returned. "How came you gentlemen to this place?"

Escott may have picked up on my uneasiness and was cautious. "I believe you heard all that was said to Miss Francher."

"So I did," he admitted. "It was I who persuaded her to allow you in. She values her privacy very much and we are naturally worried about robbery, but I was curious as to how you know Maureen Dumont. She was a friend of mine."

He watched both our reactions, his eyes moving back and forth in a way that put prickles under my collar.

"Was?" I asked, trying to keep the thickness out of my voice.

"We were once very close."

"How close?"

"I've not seen or heard from her for some five years," he said, ignoring the question and watching me.

I started to say something, but Escott stepped in instead. "Would you relate to us the exact circumstances of your last contact with her?"

He dragged his eyes from me to Escott. "Possibly, but I would first like some information about the two of you." Now his full attention was focused on Escott. "Who are you? Why are you here?"

"My name is Charles W. Escott. I am a licensed private investigator from Chicago and this is my colleague, Jack Fleming. Mr. Fleming was a very close friend of Miss Dumont. In August of 1931, Miss Dumont disappeared. This took place within a few hours of her sister Gaylen's escape—"

"Charles," I warned.

He stopped abruptly and shook his head a little. I thought he was trying to put me off.

"Go on," said our host, leaning forward.

". . . escape from a private sanatorium in—"

I looked at Escott—really *looked* at him—and the skin on my scalp started crawling every which way.

"—Kingsburg. She—"

"Charles." This time I grabbed one shoulder and turned him to face me. His gray eyes were empty. He was unaware of everything except the last question he'd heard and his absolute necessity to answer it.

"—telephoned her friend . . . telephoned . . ."

Hardly knowing what I was doing myself, I lunged at the secretary and hauled him from his chair and slammed him against the nearest wall. Escott's voice trailed off and stopped. An instant later the man's arm shot up and he caught me in the soft spot right under the rib cage. If I'd been breathing I'd have doubled over. As it was, the force of the blow surprised me and sent me staggering back into his chair.

I went right over in a crash and tangle, bruising my arm on an unpadded wooden edge. He started to come after me, but stopped short, as though undecided whether to help me up or belt me again.

"Easy now," he said, holding his hands with the palms out. I'd spoken the same way to that horse last night to keep it calm. We glared at each other for a few long seconds, and then I glanced at Escott. He was still on the couch and oblivious to what had just happened.

The man said nothing when I looked back at him. He was on guard, his white teeth showing in the kind of non-smile you see on a wolf. When I didn't leap up for another attack, he cautiously extended a hand down to me. I swatted it away before I could give in to the sudden urge to break the arm that went with it, and got to my feet without assistance.

"Easy now," he repeated. "There's no point to this, and you know it. The truth of things—that's all I wanted from him."

I knew what he was talking about, but wasn't ready to face it yet, not until Escott . . .

"Pull him out of it—and carefully, or I'll kick your ass into the sound."

"Very well," he told me. His voice was level, his rictus

smile gone, but he wouldn't hurry to do anything until he felt sure of me.

After a moment I backed off. Slowly. I wasn't under his influence, but there was little else I could do.

When he was certain I'd stay put, he crossed to Escott, looked into his eyes, and said his name. Escott blinked, as though trying hard to remember something, and came quickly back to himself. He instantly noted the tension in the room and stood up.

"What's happened?" he asked.

"We hit pay dirt," I said. "He just pulled a Lamont Cranston on you."

"Then he's . . ." Escott didn't bother to finish as the realization hit.

The man's blue eyes flickered at me and held steady like the hot part of a candle flame. "How much does *he* know about things?"

"Enough," I snapped. "Charles, you get behind me, I don't trust this son of a bitch."

Without any questions, Escott did just that. Whether he was any safer with me in front was anyone's guess.

"Jonathan," he said, recalling the secretary's name. His head cocked thoughtfully and he regarded him with abrupt understanding. "You're Jonathan Barrett."

Maureen's lover, her ageless vampire lover of three decades past, nodded once as an affirmative.

"At your service, gentlemen," he said, and smiled mirthlessly.

4

BARRETT STRAIGHTENED A little and smoothed his clothes, not taking his eyes from either of us. "I apologize for the intrusion upon you, Mr. Escott." His tone was slightly hostile and devoid of any regret. "Perhaps you will both excuse my desire to protect myself."

I said nothing, it was up to Escott to pick up the ball.

"There was no real need to influence me into giving you information."

"Yes, but then I don't know you. The information could have been false or incomplete. It saves time and trouble when both sides know where they stand. For all I knew, you might have been friends of Gaylen, not Maureen."

"What do you know about Gaylen?" I asked.

"Enough," he replied, echoing me. "How is it that you know her?"

"She was looking for Maureen and found me instead."

"And what happened to her?"

"She's no longer a threat to Maureen."

"That hardly answers my question."

I ignored the sarcastic note. "Where's Maureen?"

He studied me carefully, probably gauging my past relationship with her, perhaps even trying to see me through her eyes. That was what I was doing to him. "I don't know."

He could see I didn't believe him and said it again, spreading his hands for emphasis.

"When did you last see her, then?" asked Escott.

"On the night that Gaylen escaped from Kingsburg. She stayed for the day, departed the following dusk, and I've not heard from her or of her since then—until you two turned up to trouble my innocent employer with questions."

"How so is she innocent?"

"Miss Francher and I have a complete understanding over certain matters: I maintain her privacy and she protects mine." He turned to me. "I know you can appreciate how important privacy and discretion are to those of our nature. You should be more mindful of those dark glasses. They are a dreadful giveaway."

"Tell us about Maureen," I said.

"That's a long story."

"I've got all night and so do you."

"Of course, but I must think on where to start."

"With yourself," suggested Escott.

Barrett frowned and shook his head. "*That* would take much too long and I am not inclined this night to confess my many sins to virtual strangers."

"The primary points should be sufficient. May we begin with your life and death?"

Something like amusement seemed to light Barrett's eyes from within. "So you do know that much about us. Are you Mr. Fleming's protector?"

Escott didn't reply.

Shrugging it off as unimportant, Barrett went to the French windows and shut them against the night. "Very well. Please be seated and make yourselves comfortable. May I offer you some refreshment, Mr. Escott?"

"No, thank you."

This time Escott picked a chair off to one side of the couch. I resumed my original seat, barely settling on the edge, ready to move again if necessary. I still didn't trust the man.

Barrett righted his banker's chair, checked it for damage, and rolled it back under the desk. Apparently feeling secure about us, he sank into the opposite end of the couch from me with a mock sigh of weariness, angling against the back and arm to be able to look at us both. His loose-boned, informal posture had its effect and I felt myself relaxing a little.

"Very well," he began, looking up once at the ceiling as though searching it for the right word. "I was a lawyer's son and destined to be a lawyer as well, though I had little taste for the work. I was sent to England to study. It was my first real experience of unsupervised freedom and I quickly grew to love it. There I learned to spend my allowance in ways my father would scarce have understood, much less approved.

"Those were wild, delightful days, and the nights were made even better when I became acquainted with a certain lady of astonishing charm who taught me some unique skills in the art of love. I was but a rough, untutored colonial then, for a time I believed that that was how all men and women enjoyed themselves—I grew wiser about such things later on.

"Then war came up and I was commanded home again, that or be left without funds. Being a dutiful son, I returned. I was so dutiful that it got me killed. My father was loyal to the Crown, y'see."

"What war are you referring to?"

"The one that sundered our respective countries, Mr. Escott. The American Revolution, as it is now called." He paused to let that sink in and enjoyed our reaction.

"How old were you then?"

His eyes drifted inward, briefly. "I was not old then, Mr. Escott. I was young; very, very, young." He shifted, crossing one leg over the other. "But I was talking about the rebellion. My dear father was a Loyalist and not a damned traitor to our God-appointed sovereign. Of course, his attitude may have been tempered by the fact that Long Island was then protected by British troops. We were safe and secure from the rebels, so they said, but they couldn't be everywhere at once. I was shot down in cold blood by a pimply-faced bumpkin cowering in some trees on my father's land. The cowardly, dishonorable, half-witted bastard thought I was General Howe.''

After at least 160 years, his disgust was sincere and still fresh.

"I'll pass over the dramatic details of my death and return, and my first stumbling efforts at coping with the physical change within me. I was forever cut off from my family—if anything, I was too embarrassed to come forward and try to explain myself. By the time I'd decided to overcome it, the so-called colonial government had won their war and seized Father's property. He pulled a few pennies together and took the family back to England. I was tied to the land, though, and had to remain behind. I settled down, made a kind of life for myself, and even traveled a bit in later years when the chance presented itself.''

"How did you support yourself?" asked Escott.

"That, sir," he smiled, "is none of your business. I did a lot of reading, trying to make up for my patchy and interrupted education. Decades later, my interest in reading eventually led me to meet the Dumont sisters at some literary club. I was immediately attracted to Maureen, her feelings were in happy correspondence to my own, and nature had its course with us for many contented years.''

"What about Gaylen?" I asked.

He sighed and shook his head. "She knew something was going on; but never came out and asked anything. It worried Maureen, but there was little she could do about it. She chose to do nothing.''

"What did you do?"

"Nothing. It was Maureen's concern and up to her on how to handle things. I merely followed her wishes. Gaylen was a strange woman. There were no doctors then who could be of any help to her. She was too clever to be obviously mad.''

"What was she like?"

"Strange," he repeated unhelpfully. "Normal on the outside, but there was a soft and rotten core of sickness within that never showed itself until you really got to know her. She liked to use people, but only in petty ways, mind you. She'd never put on a manner to make you think she was imposing on your goodwill."

"What do you mean?"

"There are some people you like to do things for, simply because they're nice and know how to say thank you. On the surface, Gaylen seemed to be one of them. She was pleasant company, and careful never to go too far, but she was really using people in her own way. As an outsider to their family with some larger experience, I could see how she worked all things around her to her favor . . . oh, but she was ever so nice about it.

"Maureen did everything she could for her, but it was never enough. Gaylen enjoyed playing the sweet suffering martyr and craved the attention it got her. In later years, Gaylen practically clung to Maureen, 'as if increase of appetite had grown by what it fed on,' if I may borrow from the bard. When Maureen had her accident, it was too much for Gaylen; she completely fell apart."

"The accident that killed her?"

"Yes. She told you about the fire wagon? I'm surprised; she hated talking about it, even thinking about it made her feel sick."

Having suffered a violent death myself, I could understand.

"For me it was a miracle. I hadn't lost her to death. She'd come back to me, beautiful as ever, and young again. I helped her through her first nights, easing things when I could, but after a time she found she couldn't let go. She wanted to go back, to comfort Gaylen and to let her know she was really all right."

His expression had turned inward again; he was half-sad, half-angry. "It was a mistake and a very bad one, but she couldn't see it at first. She talked me into helping—pleaded, really—it was that important to her. So I helped. It was all right for a time, but when the happy shock of the reunion wore off and the implications sank in, Gaylen started to work on us both. She was slow and subtle about it, but she wanted to be like us. She said there was every chance of the change working in her since they were sisters."

"She couldn't talk either of you into it, though."

"It wasn't for want of trying, and finally she tried too hard. That was her mistake; that's when Maureen realized how sick her sister was in her mind. Things got very ugly, very fast after that scene, and she had to put Gaylen away in Kingsburg, which all but broke Maureen's heart. Gaylen was the cause of the rift between us; thereafter Maureen and I went on separate paths."

"But you kept in touch?"

"Out of mutual self-interest and because of what we'd become. Those of our kind are despairingly rare." His glance rested on me a moment and I couldn't read his expression.

"What self-interest?"

"Gaylen was full of mischief and I had little confidence in the security of that so-called asylum. Bedlam may have been noisy, brutal, and stunk to high heaven, but they knew how to keep a door locked. We each had to know where the other lived in case something happened—which it did when she escaped."

"Who paid for the asylum?"

"Maureen. She and Gaylen inherited enough from their parents to live in quiet comfort for the rest of their lives. When Maureen understood how things might be for her future with me, she made out a rather clever will that gave over her share of the estate to a nonexistent cousin. If the cousin did not appear within a year of her demise, then her share would go to Gaylen. It was easy enough to establish another identity in those days, and my background in law was proving to be quite handy for once. Maureen prepared for her change—if it happened, and so it did.''

"It surprised you?"

"I was truthful with her. I told her there was no guarantee she would rise again; it was only a chance and we took it.''

Escott stirred in his chair. "And the others?''

"What do you mean, sir?''

"Since your decease you must have been involved with women other than Maureen.''

Barrett was amused. "Of course I was. I'd changed, but not into a damned monk.''

"Did any of them return after they died?''

He didn't answer, but Escott continued to wait for one. "No, none of them,'' he said with a flare of anger. "Not one of them. D'ye want to know how many there were and all that we did together?''

Escott ignored the question. "What about the lady you knew in England? What was her story?''

"I was her lover, not her bloody biographer.''

Escott was patient, which irritated Barrett.

"Her name was Nora Jones and she made her living by accepting such gifts as we lads could afford to give her, but mind you, she was no whore—don't ever think that. She was a lovely girl, truly lovely and lovable. Not all the students were poor, and I was doubly blessed with a bit of paternal lucre and good looks, both of which she took to like butter to warm bread.''

"Did she not warn you of the possible consequences of her relationship with you?''

"No, she did not. It was her way; she liked 'em young and fairly innocent, and was pleased to keep 'em so. I've also come to think that she honestly did not know there would even be consequences.''

"Your resurrection must have been quite traumatic for you.''

His face grew hard at the memory. "It was, and I'd rather not speak of it."

"Then we shall return to the near-present: tell us about the night Maureen came here to you."

"There's little enough to tell. I'd obtained a position here some months earlier as Miss Francher's secretary. As you're already aware by now, she knows all about me, but however odd the hours might be, I am very good at my job."

"And it's safe here," I added.

He considered the remark. "Yes, as safe as one can be from life. We had our share of ill fortune that year. Miss Francher's mother died horribly in a fire that spring and I had my hands full for a time, helping her get through the worst of it and protecting her privacy. If not for young Laura it would have been impossible. She was only fourteen then, but a splendid child; the experience matured and strengthened her even as it seemed to drain her older cousin. She'd been visiting us on her spring holiday that week and then stayed on. I arranged for a private tutor so she could finish out the year at home with us."

"What about Laura's family?"

"Her parents died ten years ago. Miss Francher's mother was her legal guardian. When she died, Miss Francher assumed the responsibility. It was easy enough, for Laura is a good girl. Things were just starting to settle down at the close of summer when Maureen showed up at the gate asking for me. She was in quite a state about Gaylen and hardly able to think straight. I'd said that things had gotten very ugly between them, she was afraid of what her sister might do to her. She wanted help and advice, and I offered what little I could."

"Which was?"

"I said she should set the police to watching her flat and to keep herself out of sight until they caught the old girl again. It seemed the most obvious thing to do, but she was that panicked."

"Did Miss Francher know of this?"

"I saw no need to trouble her with my personal problems. I told her Maureen was an old friend dropping by for a visit and she was content with that."

It sounded as though Emily Francher had been remarkably accommodating for one who demanded such privacy, and I speculated that he might have influenced her into her contentment. "How long did Maureen stay?"

"She didn't. I invited her to remain as long as she liked until they found Gaylen, and she accepted. With a place this big, there are any number of rooms she'd be safe and comfortable in, especially my own, which is well locked and fireproofed. The servants have standing orders never to go inside and they are paid enough not to be overly curious."

"Convenient." Again, I figured he'd have insured himself by slipping them some quiet suggestions on the side.

"Indeed. Maureen turned down the offer and picked another room. I saw that she was settled, did some work of my own, and stopped by to say good night and to see if she needed anything. She did not, so I went to bed."

"You saw her?"

"I called through the door and she answered."

That struck us both as odd and he knew it.

"She didn't really want to see me," he admitted.

"Why's that?" I asked.

"We had a disagreement, more of a quiet fight, really. She didn't approve of my job and I told her it was none of her business how I chose to live. Things rapidly deteriorated from there."

"And she still accepted your invitation to stay the day?"

"By then it was too late for her to go elsewhere; the time had gotten away from us. She stayed, but left right after sunset the next night. By the time I was up and about, she was gone."

"Without a good-bye?"

"Or even a thank-you. She must have been very angry with

me, but then I was hardly feeling like a good Christian toward her myself.''

''How did she leave?''

''Same as she came; by taxi.''

''Do you know where she went?''

''No.''

''Anyone else see her leave?''

''Mayfair—that's the gardener—had to let them in and out. You may ask him if you like, though I warn you he's got a brain like a block of Swiss cheese.''

''And you never tried to contact her?''

''I called her flat a few times, but she was never home. Later on when I called, someone else had rented the place. She never called or wrote, I expect she never wanted to see me again.'' He'd drifted away, as though he were talking to himself. I wasn't the only one Maureen had hurt.

''Did you ever think that Gaylen might have found her?''

''Not seriously, no. Once Maureen had a little time to get over her upset, I knew she'd be able to take care of herself.''

''Was your disagreement serious enough for her to cut you off just like that?''

''I suppose it was, from her point of view. No woman likes to see herself supplanted by another in a man's heart, even a man she's long ago discarded.''

''Are you referring to your employer?'' asked Escott in that carefully neutral tone of his, which meant he thought his question was important.

Barrett fastened him with a cold eye. ''As I told Maureen, *that* is none of your business.''

Escott dropped the subject for another. ''What about the phone call for Maureen you received the next night?''

''Call?''

''From her friend. Maureen gave her the number of this house as though she expected to be here for a time.''

''Oh, that. I remember.''

"You gave this person the impression Maureen was still here."

"I think I offered to take a message and I wanted to know who was calling. I was curious and I thought she might be involved with Gaylen in some way. Who was it?"

"She was not involved with Gaylen and she asked that we not mention her name."

He shrugged, uninterested.

"Are you not curious about Maureen and what happened to her?"

"Of course I am, why d'ye think I got the two of you in here to start with? A lot of good it's done me since you've no news of her—or have you?"

"Regrettably, we do not."

"That's no surprise." He turned his attention to me. "How well did you know her?"

"Very well."

"That's evident, laddie. You must have been something special to her altogether. So why hasn't she tried to contact you, eh? Had a fight with her, too?"

"She left to protect me from Gaylen, that's all I know."

"And you said you met Gaylen?"

"She met me."

"What about her? Did the asylum finally catch up with her? You said she was caught?"

I glanced at Escott. He left it up to me. "I said she was no longer a threat. She's dead."

He thought it over for a time, reading more off my face than I felt comfortable about. "How, then, did it happen? How did she come to find you?"

"It doesn't matter, she just did. She thought I might know where Maureen was, but I couldn't help her."

"Perhaps not to find Maureen, maybe she wanted your help in other ways—and don't look so dark, laddie, I knew her, too, and far better. I knew what she wanted and how badly she wanted it, and if you turned her down, I shan't think ill of you. I said she was sick. Sometimes death is the best cure for her kind of misery. You *did* turn her down? She really is dead?"

"She is," confirmed Escott. "Heart failure."

I felt my face twisting in reaction. Maybe not all of the nightmare had left; something perverse inside me wanted to laugh. I got up and walked to the French windows instead. The pool lights were out and the blond swimmer was long gone. The water was still and smooth.

"Death is the best cure sometimes," Barrett repeated. "It keeps her from passing her sickness on to others and making them miserable in turn. One can hope for as much at least."

Some distance beyond the pool was a bare, fenced yard with a few trees in it and the dark, rounded shapes of horses dozing on their feet. No doubt they were part of Barrett's food supply. It was very convenient and comfortable for him to have such an obliging patroness.

I could understand Maureen's reaction to it all. In her day she had been well off and certainly attractive. Then Barrett came into her life, offering her love and a possibility of eternal youth in exchange for her money and protection. It *could* have been that way, an old story with a new twist that Barrett apparently repeated if he had the same arrangement with Emily Francher. No wonder Maureen had been upset, but I didn't think she'd have simply gone off without a final word to him. She had manners as well, she would have surely left him some kind of a note.

I turned back into the room. They were both looking at me; Escott alert and Barrett . . . watchful. I focused my full attention on him, freezing hard onto his brilliant eyes, reaching into his mind.

"Where is Maureen? Tell me."

Escott held his breath. There was total silence except for his heart thudding a little faster than normal.

"You know how to find her," I said. "Where is she?"

Barrett looked slightly surprised, not blank, as I'd expected.

"Tell me."

His face darkened.

"Where is she?"

He stood up to face me square on: a tall man, well built, wearing modern, elegant clothes. Hard, primitive fury flooded and marred his features. I'd done exactly the wrong thing by trying to influence an answer from him.

His hands had worked into fists. He made an effort to keep his voice steady.

"I have already told you I do not know where she is." He was shaking from his anger, but holding himself carefully in check. "And remember this, Fleming, no one has ever called me a liar and lived. . . . Keep that in mind before you say aught else."

Something moved out in the hall, a light footstep as someone passed the door. Escott started breathing again, but his heart was still thumping very fast. It was just distracting enough, so I did think twice about my next words and it was damned difficult to get them out.

"If . . . *if* you should ever see her again—" I paused, but he held back, listening "—tell her Gaylen is dead. Tell her I only want to know that she's all right." My mouth was very dry. "If she doesn't want to see me again, I'll respect her decision."

Barrett was a perceptive man; he could see what it had cost me to say that. His expression softened and he gave a slight nod. "And you'll do the same for me?"

"Yes."

He nodded again. "If I should ever see her again, I will tell her that for you. *If* . . ."

And he left that last word hanging in the air between us with all its attendant uncertainty and doubt.

* * *

Our car rumbled slowly down the drive, gravel spreading and crunching under the tires as we followed the gardener's truck to the front gate.

"What do you think?" I asked Escott.

He replied with a shake of the head.

Fair enough, I felt about the same. "I can't believe the trail stops here."

We rounded the turn at the side of the non-ruins of the old house and rolled gently downhill at a slightly faster speed. The truck was now nearly up to ten miles an hour.

"Got any questions for Johnny Appleseed up ahead?"

"If you mean the gardener, yes, I have. As for Barrett, he said much that agreed with what we heard from Gaylen—the manner of Maureen's death, her separation from Barrett—on those points we can assume he was being truthful."

"And of Maureen coming here and leaving?"

"I don't know. Her abrupt departure is just odd enough as a story to be true. He could just as easily have told us something more plausible. Having never met her, I do not know if such behavior is something you'd expect from her. Is it?"

"She left me, didn't she?" Like a spectator standing apart, I noticed the bitter tone in my voice. Escott remained mercifully silent.

The gardener got out to open the front gate for us. Escott followed him and cornered the man. His wife appeared on the porch of the gatehouse and glared at them both, but Escott had anticipated her and carefully maneuvered the man so he was unaware of her presence.

Escott talked and got some mumbled replies along with head scratching, head shaking, and shrugs until the fellow caught sight of his better half and decided it was past time to go inside. Escott shook hands with him briefly. From the look that passed between them I knew he'd given him a private tip for his help, such as it was.

We drove out. Escott waved at him and got a guarded half wave in return.

"What'd he say?"

"A moment," he said, and a quarter-mile later pulled the car onto the road shoulder and cut the motor. "Lord, but that place was oppressive."

"And I thought it was just me."

My answer had to wait more than a moment as he got out his pipe, tobacco pouch, and matches. Soon he was successfully drawing smoke into his lungs and filling the car up with the aromatic exhaust. The excess floated out the windows into the cool night air of the woods around us.

He looked at the pale gray swirl without really seeing it. "Mr. Mayfair confirmed Barrett's story. It was a memorable spring because of the fire and death of Mrs. Francher, but things were more or less back to normal by summer. Unlike her mother, Miss Francher did not encourage visitors, and after her views were made quite clear to her various relatives, they ceased to call. Young Laura was the only one she'd have anything to do with. Again, he confirmed Barrett's statement that Emily took over the girl's guardianship."

"Did he remember Maureen?"

"Not by name, but he did recall admitting a young woman on Barrett's authority that summer. The circumstances were similar enough to our own arrival to bring the incident readily to mind. She arrived in a Green Light cab one night and departed the next, also by cab; a local called out from the nearest town."

"Green Light is based in Manhattan."

"Mr. Mayfair was aware of that at the time, which was another unusual detail for him to remember. He'd spent some thought on speculating how high the fare had been."

"Great. What else?"

"Nothing more to concern us, I'm afraid. Aside from the expected traffic of tradesmen, the only other visitors of note were the demolition men charged with the task of tearing down the burned shell of the old house."

"Can we try tracing the local cab?"

"I'll have a go at it first thing tomorrow," he promised. "Now about tonight . . ."

"What about it?"

"Our interview was fascinating, but I felt a bit short-changed on actual facts about the household. I want to ask if you would mind returning to the house tonight."

"What? Pull a peeping-tom act?"

"Engage in further investigation," he corrected mildly. "I also cannot believe the trail stops here and would like to know more about the place and the people in it. I'm interested in the cars they possess and who actually owns them. How many servants do they employ? Do any of them actually live in the house? Barrett mentioned he had a secure resting place; where is it?"

"Oh, is that all?"

He chose to overlook the touch of sarcasm. "Any piece of information, no matter how trivial, may be of value."

"And if Barrett catches me?"

"See that he doesn't."

▲
5
▼

IT WAS EASY for him to say, he didn't have to go over the brick wall up the road and bumble through the woods to reach the house—not that that was too much trouble. Most of the time I was incorporeal, and passed over the terrain the way Escott's pipe smoke drifted out the car window. In a bodiless state the wall was no problem, and my clothes were spared the rigors of a hike through the wilderness. I just didn't like my errand or anything to do with it; I was looking for things to complain about.

I had to pause and re-form often to get my bearings, but I made good speed, swiftly flowing between the solid bulk of the tree trunks until I was within spitting distance of the garage. After that I took my time. Barrett's night vision was equal to my own, and unlike normal humans he could spot me in my invisible state.

Creeping into the garage, I checked each of the cars: an early Ford on blocks, a Rolls, a Caddy, and a brand-new white Studebaker. I dutifully wrote their plate numbers in my notebook and looked over their paperwork. All of them were owned by Emily Francher.

The floor above the garage was occupied by two women, both comfortably asleep. They had separate rooms, but shared a bath and had black uniforms hanging in the closets that identified them as regular staff. I picked gingerly through their purses to get their names, and ghosted outside again without disturbing them. As a vampire hell-bent on finding slumbering maidens to drain into terminal anemia, I was a total washout.

The stables were next, and were just as quiet. The horses may have been used to late-night visits. Two stood in stalls and six more wandered loose in the adjoining corral. None of them did more than cock an interested ear in my direction.

Upstairs, a section had been converted to living quarters, and I found a young man happily snoring away in his bed. His place was cluttered with horsey-smelling clothes, riding boots in both English and Western styles, and other related junk. He had a modest collection of Zane Grey novels on a shelf and below them was a pile of magazines whose pictured contents were anything but modest. Again, I quietly raided a wallet for identification.

The easy stuff out of the way, I oozed through the back door of the main house and solidified in the kitchen. A small light over one of the electric stoves kept it from being totally dark. Various doors opened to a hall, the dining room, pantry, and the basement. I picked the basement, changed to a semi-transparent state for silence and speed, and sailed down the stairs.

The walls were very solid concrete and the massive house above was well supported by a forest of thick pillars. I went solid for a moment and listened, but caught only the irregular drip of water from the laundry room. A slightly musty smell hung in the still air, coming from some odd pieces of old furniture stacked against a brick wall opposite the stairs. It was only a basement and a waste of my time.

I was halfway back to the kitchen when it hit me: the place was much too small. I went down again and checked the brickwork. Not being an expert, I couldn't tell if it was part of the original building or not, but my curiosity was up. I disappeared and pushed forward through the bricks.

It was slow work, like walking through sticky oatmeal. I

didn't like the feeling at all and the wall was nearly a foot thick. It seemed like forever before I tumbled into free and open space again, to re-form for a look around.

On this side the bricks were hidden by fine oak paneling, and the utilitarian presence of the support pillars had been softened by similar decoration. Some of them had been converted into four-sided bookshelves, each loaded with hundreds of titles. A thick rug covered most of the parquet flooring and several lamps held back the darkness. The chairs and sofas looked comfortable and the air was fresh.

Barrett had done very well for himself.

He'd said his room was fireproof and secure, qualities which struck me as wise precautions. It was no wonder vampires had a reputation for hanging around graveyards; few things are more fireproof or private than a stone mausoleum. But this basement location was a real luxury and far better than anything I might have planned for myself. I was frankly envious.

The entrance to his sanctum was a heavy industrial-type metal door covered in more wood paneling. It led to a carpeted hall and a flight of steps going up to a door with access to the ground floor. Both were locked, which was sensible. I went back down again and got nosy.

His quarters consisted of a large living area, bedroom, bath, and a good-sized closet. The bed was unusually large, with a fancy embroidered canopy. It was for use, not for show, since the nightstand held some personal clutter. His carpet slippers lay jumbled on the floor next to it.

I cautiously looked under the brocaded blue bedspread and plain white sheets and found a doubled thickness of oilcloth stretched over the mattress. It was sewn shut at the edges, but I could tell by the weight and feel that it contained his home earth. It was a very neat arrangement, one that I intended to adapt for myself, now that I had the idea.

Beyond the bedroom was a spotless white-tiled bath, supplied with the usual appointments, except that the cabinet over the sink lacked a mirror. It was an easily understandable omission.

His closet was stocked with a number of suits. He favored dark blues and grays for his business wear, had two tuxedos, and some riding gear. One long rack contained a rainbow of shirts, ties, and handkerchiefs. Almost everything was silk.

At the back of the closet was a big antique trunk. It was banged up, but in good, solid condition. It was also locked, but I could guess he had a spare supply of earth inside in case he felt a need to travel.

I heard a footfall just outside the room and damn near panicked.

Stupidly, I had an idea he'd use a key, but he no more needed a key than I did. He had slipped inside the same silent way. I froze absolutely still, afraid he'd hear my eyelids blinking. I could certainly hear his every movement. Two soft thumps indicated he'd removed his shoes and other, less distinct sounds I interpreted as him undressing. I had a wild hope he wouldn't bother with the closet and abruptly discarded it as he padded my way.

Abject fear can be inspiring; I made a fast and wild-eyed search for a hiding place and spotted a ventilation grate in the ceiling. In the time it took for him to grasp the knob of the closet door and swing it open, I'd vanished and swept up into the narrow shaft.

Even in a disembodied state it was uncomfortable, and I had some very unpleasant thoughts that it might lead to the furnace. I'm not usually claustrophobic, but a few minutes of such close confinement was more than enough for my rattled brain. I couldn't go back to the closet, but if I didn't get out soon, my attack of mental sweats would send me solid again. Since the shaft seemed to be only ten inches square, that was the last thing I wanted to happen.

I flowed along the metal tunnel, felt an upward turning, and took it, hoping for the best and trying not to think about furnaces. After that I got lost; in this non-physical state it's almost impossible to avoid. It's like turning somersaults underwater with your eyes shut. Before too long you lose all sense of direction and can surface for air only to bump against the bottom of the pond.

I streamed along, just barely maintaining control, and suddenly sieved into open space again, which was a great improvement. By extended touch I made out the shapes of large unyielding surfaces and guessed them to be furnishings. I slowly re-formed and found my guess to be correct. The room was unoccupied; I sank into a chair and spent awhile pulling my nerves together. The next time Escott wanted information he could damn well get it himself. Playing the rabbit in a tunnel was not my idea of fun.

After a few minutes of quiet, I was settled down enough to move on and find out where I'd ended up. A look out a window confirmed that I was on the second floor overlooking the front lawn, though I wasn't close to any inhabited areas. The rooms I checked were dark and very much underfurnished. It didn't seem to be from any lack of money, simply lack of interest. The house had been built for socializing and entertaining lots of guests, something Emily Francher actively avoided. I wondered why her mother had turned down such a gift.

Down one long hall I discovered Emily's suite of rooms, and like Barrett, she'd indulged in every comfort and convenience. More French windows opened onto the back veranda and were so heavily curtained as to be lightproof. If she stayed up to keep Barrett company at night, she was likely to be a very late sleeper, but just to be sure I checked under the bedclothes. No oilcloth flats of earth lurked beneath the sheets. Emily was quite human and during the day she slept alone.

Her favorite colors were red, gold, and white; the decor was expensive, of course, but not overpowering. I poked through drawers and found clothes and vanity items, but nothing useful like a soul-revealing diary. The bedside table contained a Bible, several used-up crossword-puzzle books, pencils, a copy of *Anthony Adverse*, and a big, nearly full bottle of sleeping pills.

Her walk-in closet was larger than Barrett's, held enough clothes to open a store, but even my uneducated male eye could tell many of them were years out of style. Two heavy-looking cases in one corner caught my attention. One was open and contained those few pieces of jewelry she hadn't worn tonight: a couple of gold bracelets, some rings, and a pearl necklace. The other case was locked and wouldn't budge. On closer look both proved to be made of thick metal covered with wood veneer and welded to a huge metal plate bolted to the floor. Emily was careless, but not completely stupid.

Leaving her room, I moved down the hall and invaded Barrett's private office. The rolltop part of the desk was locked and I couldn't open it without making a lot of noise and leaving traces. The drawers were open, but only contained the usual supplies. If neatness counted for anything, Barrett earned his keep well enough.

I was starting down the central stairs to the front hall and nearly blundered into him again. A door below opened and shut, followed by swift, decisive footsteps. Backing up the stairs, I crouched behind the railings, keeping very still. He emerged into view, his bootheels making a clatter against the marble floor as he crossed the hall to the parlor. As for the rest of his clothes . . . I felt my jaw sag open.

The hall was too open and dangerous; I opted to slip outside again and moved around to the front to peer in through the parlor window. The curtains were thin enough; I very much wanted to get a second look at the man.

The lamp was off and the only light now came from the fireplace. Emily Francher had moved from her chair to a long settee, where she reclined, still clad in her diamonds and red velvet. For the first time I noticed the high waist on her garment, and it made me think of something from the Napoleonic era. The soft glow from the fire added to the illusion of the far past.

Barrett was leaning against the mantel. My initial glimpse hadn't been any hallucination; he'd changed his business suit for a costume from a long-lost century. He wore a flowing, open-necked white shirt with loose, full sleeves, some form-fitting riding pants, and a supple pair of boots. All he needed now was a fancy coat and sword, or maybe a brace of dueling pistols to complete the effect. With his thick hair now carelessly tumbling over his forehead, he looked like a friendlier version of Brontë's Heathcliff.

The intervening glass muffled things a little, but I had no trouble making out their voices.

"I don't think they'll be back," he was saying to her. "They just had a few questions about someone I once knew."

"What about her?" she asked. "That young man seemed very anxious to find her."

He shook his head. "I think they'll look elsewhere now."

"You're still troubled."

"Only because I don't want them to come back. I don't want them bothering you."

"My protector," she said, and broke into a sudden smile. It transformed her face and I could see strong evidence of the pretty young woman she had once been. He smiled as well and came to kneel on one knee next to her, taking one of her hands in both of his. Her eyes clouded with doubt. "Will it be different for us, do you think?"

He kissed her hand quickly, reassuringly. "I certainly hope so, dearest. I will do everything possible to make it so for you." He caressed her face tenderly and kissed her forehead. "I promise."

"Really?" The playfulness was back in her expression.

"I'll show you."

He undid her choker necklace and kissed her forehead again, then her eyes, then her mouth. His arms half lifted her from the settee, pulling her body close to his own. Her head tilted back and he moved lower, his lips closing possessively over the two faint marks on her throat that the choker had concealed.

Her own arms were wrapped tightly around him, one hand pressing on the back of his neck to help guide him to that special spot. His jaw worked and a tremor ran through her whole body in response. He stayed there, drinking from her, for what seemed a very long time.

My conscience was working a blue streak. How do you know where to draw the line between curiosity and voyeurism? I went transparent, pushed away into the darkness beyond the window, and floated around the corner of the house.

That they were lovers was no stunning surprise. Their style of going about it was much more sedate than some of the wild tumbles that Bobbi and I had shared, but to each his own. Despite their quiet method, the passion was there, and I could sympathize with it enough to get stirred up myself, but Bobbi was nearly eight hundred miles away. As for the horses in the backyard—they were for food, not sex. There is a very decided difference between the two, at least for me. I'd just have to hike around in the woods until the pleasant frustration wore off, and try to make up for it when I got back to Chicago. Bobbi wouldn't mind.

The other thing bothering me was Barrett's wish for us to stay away. Maybe he was afraid we'd be rocking the sweet little boat he'd gotten for himself as Emily Francher's secretary. On the other hand, he'd have to be a better actor than Escott if that love scene I'd just watched had been a fake. If he genuinely loved her, then he'd want to protect her from his past indiscretions and present troubles. Put in his place, I'd be doing the same.

Then there was Emily Francher wondering if things would be different for them. Was she talking about a better relationship than he'd had with Maureen or whether Barrett's attentions would bring her back when she died? I was inclined to think it was the latter, since she didn't seem to know all that much about Maureen.

Note that word—*seem*. Being lousy at lying myself often made me vulnerable to the lies of others. But right now I was too interested in finding Maureen to want to give anyone the benefit of a doubt.

The sound of radio music eventually tugged me out of my thoughts. It came from some open French windows on the second floor and reminded me that there was at least one other member of the household.

I drifted up and steadied myself with a ghostly hand on the veranda railing just outside the fan of light filtering through the lacy white curtains.

Laura Francher, the lithe blond I'd seen swimming in the pool below, was before a large mirror that nearly covered one wall of her bedroom. A balance bar ran in front of it at waist height, but she wasn't bothering with any ballet practice at the moment. Instead, she was swaying to the music of Rudy Vallee; her eyes shut as she danced with a pretend partner. Her feet were bare, but then so was the rest of her.

I hung back in the shadows and settled into solidity again. I only wanted to be able to hear the radio better. Honest.

I noted with quick interest that she was a natural blond. It was certainly fascinating, but I didn't think Escott would find that particular detail of much use in our investigation. My conscience was trying to kick up again, though at times I could be selectively deaf to it. What a pretty girl did to occupy herself alone in her room was her business—but the view was *very* absorbing. I reflected that this kind of detecting could easily become addictive. I'd give myself just one more minute and then move on.

When the minute ran out, Rudy was still singing and by then I was speculating what she'd look like performing a fast rumba when she abruptly stopped and scampered to a closet. She emerged a second later, hastily belting up a bright yellow bathrobe. Smoothing down her long hair, she opened the door.

It was Barrett and she let him in.

He was still in his poet's costume and looking less relaxed than he'd been with Emily. The whites of his eyes were solid red, still suffused with her blood. Their condition didn't seem to bother Laura, who shut the door behind him readily enough. The radio continued to blare, which was bad for me since I couldn't hear a word of their conversation. It was like watching a play through a telescope.

Barrett was obviously uncomfortable, but Laura appeared not to notice and settled in at her dressing table to brush out her thick, straight hair. Her loosely tied bathrobe was starting to come apart with the activity. She didn't bother to correct things. Barrett had called her a child, and so she must have been five years ago—not anymore. Her every movement indicated the confident maturity of a young woman who knows she is desirable.

He gently took the hairbrush from her hand, wanting her undivided attention. He'd finally worked himself up to say something, and it seemed pretty important. I ground my teeth, wishing I could read lips.

As he spoke, Laura's face grew cool and lost all expression. She studied her reflection in the mirror above the table. Barretts' own lack of reflection in it was nothing new to her, either. He ran out of words eventually and waited for some reaction. Rudy was replaced by Bing Crosby before the girl smiled and sighed out a reply.

Barretts' mouth opened; he was surprised and relieved at once. Their talk continued, apparently along the lines of questions and reassurances until both were smiling. He relaxed, lighter looking now that his errand was out of the way, and watched as she retrieved her brush and resumed work on her hair.

Her robe was still more than a little loose and her movements opened it wider. He spoke to her and she looked up and smiled at his concern. She had wonderfully large eyes, the kind that were made for men to get lost in. For all his age and experience, Barrett was no less vulnerable to them than anyone else, myself included. His hand went out and softly stroked the length of her shining hair.

She liked it but was content only to look at him and to wait for his next move. He obviously wanted her, his expression made that plain enough, but not just yet. He stood up, murmured something, and let himself out the door. She stared after him, then turned back to the mirror to smile patiently at herself. As far as she was concerned, his upcoming seduction was a foregone conclusion.

The car was at a slight tilt where it rested off the shoulder of the road. The night-shadowed landscape beyond the windshield looked askew from where I was sitting, which more or less suited my state of mind.

I talked and Escott smoked and listened, getting an earful. My description of the house and staff lacked for no detail, but when I got around to Barrett's relationship with Emily and Laura, I did some self-conscious editing. Escott noticed, but chose not to comment on what was left out, and kept puffing on his pipe. He continued to do so long after I'd wound down and stopped.

"Well?" I asked. The crickets out in the woods had held the floor long enough. "What do you think?"

His pipe had gone dead. Frowning absently, he tapped it empty and pocketed it for the time being. "I think this needs more study," he stated.

"More study?"

"But you've done some excellent groundwork." He paged through my scribbled notes, looking at each name. "I'll get busy with these tomorrow and try to follow up on the destination of Maureen's departing cab."

He saw my disappointment and added, "Our other alternative is to wait indefinitely on Barrett."

We'd given him the name of our Manhattan hotel and the mailing address in Chicago so he could send us word of Maureen. To me, it was nothing more than manners with no substance. We went through the motions, but I didn't believe anything would come of it.

"The hell with that," I growled.

Escott nodded agreement and started the car.

The next night I woke up in a strange room, which is very disorienting when you don't expect it, and I didn't.

My trunk was shoved against a wall too close for the lid to hinge back so I had to sieve my way out. I spent a few seconds gaping at the change of scene, then called to Escott to demand an explanation, except he wasn't there to provide one. He hadn't left a note, but since his suitcase was making creases in the homemade quilt on one of the tidy beds, it was reasonable to expect him back sometime soon. He knew my habits.

I was surrounded by dark, heavy furniture, old-fashioned wallpaper, framed scenes of us winning the American Revolution, and handmade rugs. Outside and one story down were huge trees, a gravel drive, cut lawn, fresh air, and a picturesque white picket fence. We were probably not in Manhattan.

The stationery on a tall bureau introduced me to the Glenbriar Inn of Glenbriar, Long Island, and a thin brochure pointed out sites of historical interest. It was so absorbing I dropped it flat the second Escott keyed the door and walked in.

"I was a bit delayed," he apologized. "I'd hoped to be back earlier in order to soften the shock."

"Too bad, I've used up all my double takes for the night. You missed a beaut when I came out and found this. What's with the move?"

"I thought it necessary and more convenient to the investigation if we could be closer to the Francher estate. This village happens to be where they do most of their local business."

"It must have been a million laughs getting me and the trunk upstairs."

"I had help, but I'd rather not go into details at the present." Slowly and painfully, he stretched out on the other, uncluttered bed, and I noticed that he was looking very green at the edges.

"You all right?"

"As well as can be expected after imbibing large amounts of coffee, tea, and beer, mixed with sweetbreads, biscuits, pretzels, and salted nuts."

I looked down with sympathetic horror. He managed not to groan or clutch his aching stomach, though he had every right to do so.

"Any reason why you put away all that stuff, or do you just go into a fit now and then?"

"The tearooms, inns, and pubs of this tour-minded place require plenty of custom if you expect to learn any of the local gossip. Did you know William Cullen Bryant used to live not far from here? They have a pair of his spectacles on display in a tearoom museum, which was urgently recommended to me as a pleasant diversion for the day."

"His spectacles?" I echoed, trying to sound impressed.

"Indeed."

"Well, well. Who'd have thought it?"

"Indeed."

"Charles . . ."

He raised one hand so I could bear with him one more time. "Tell me, *who* was William Cullen Bryant?"

"Editor of the *New York Evening Post* back in the last century."

"No relation to the orator of the Scopes trial?"

"That was William Jennings Bryan, not Bryant." I wondered just how much he'd had to drink.

He shut his eyes and gave in to a shudder. "Have you ever

tried to turn a conversation around from spectacles to house fires?''

I admitted that I'd never had the opportunity.

''It does require some skill in order not to get caught at it. If people sense you are eager to learn something specific, you end up with too much information or none at all. Let them talk on their own and you learn everything you need.''

''How can you have too much information?''

''Many feel the plain truth is too plain and requires embroidery.''

''Does this mean you got more dope on the Franchers?''

''A good deal, mixed up with a half dozen other families, but the fire was an excellent point on which to focus their attention. It was quite the nine-day wonder, and once the subject had been introduced, one thing led to another.''

''So tell me already.''

Eyes shut and hands cradling his head, he began talking to the ceiling. ''Violet Francher, the mother who died in the fire, was quite the proper and respectable dowager, but of the sort best admired from a distance. She had a sharp tongue, a temper bordering on the apoplectic, and I need hardly mention she had a difficult time keeping servants for very long.

''She was alone the night of the fire, as her housekeeper left her employ some three days earlier. Daughter Emily, ward Laura, and Mr. Barrett were all at their own house. Laura usually stayed with Violet during her spring holiday from school, but had moved in with Emily until a new housekeeper could be hired. The general consensus is the girl was very lucky, or she might have died along with her guardian.''

''It took place at night?''

''I'm glad you noticed that. I found it of extreme interest in conjunction with some other facts.''

''What are they?''

''I'm coming to them.''

''Why wasn't the old lady at the daughter's house as well?''

''I'm coming to that, too. Sometime in January—this is in

1931—Emily hired Mr. Jonathan Barrett as her secretary. They met at a party given by Violet, who still attempted to maintain some touch with society. Barrett came as a guest of a guest, had no real references, but was obviously educated and cultured. Not long after his hiring, the rumors started that something was 'going on' between him and Emily. They circulated the servants' hall and into the town and eventually made their way back to Violet, who was all moral outrage.

"She immediately made her views known in considerable detail to her daughter, and the upshot was that Barrett had to go. Much to her shock and surprise, Emily flatly refused. For the next few months, neither woman spoke to the other, and when they did, they were usually trading salvos over Barrett."

"How did he handle all this?"

"He kept in the neutral background as much as possible. He turned down the most outrageous bribes, though the question was raised as to whether Violet actually had the money. He survived the investigations of a private detective hired to find something, anything from his past that might be used to influence Emily against him—"

"What about his influence on Emily?"

He got my double meaning. "Hypnosis is a possibility, but I put much stock in the fact that Emily was genuinely in love with him. Your report of last night's rendezvous makes that a virtual certainty."

"Unless they were both faking it."

"Granted, but to return—"

"Yeah, go ahead."

"All her efforts having failed to budge him, Violet assembled a trio of psychiatrists in need of funds for the purpose of having Emily declared mentally incompetent—"

"What?"

"A tactic that had every chance of working. After all, Emily did suffer one nervous breakdown years ago, why should she not suffer another?"

"Suffer is right, her mother must have been . . ." I was at a loss. Calling her crazy didn't seem strong enough.

"Right round the twist?" he queried. "Agreed. This was a woman who wanted and usually did exercise total control over those around her—particularly over her daughter."

"So what happened with the doctors?"

"It all fell through because of the fire and her death."

"Very convenient for Barrett."

"Yes, and something else struck me as convenient and suggestively odd: in the newspaper accounts of the fire not one of them mentions his name."

I chewed that one over. "He'd naturally want a low profile. . . ."

"Low to nonexistent. Also, there was no gossip connecting him to the tragedy. If anything, some people felt Violet had brought it upon herself—'God's judgment' for having such a foul temper and that sort of thing."

"But you think he did it?"

"I think," he said after a moment, "that if it was not an accident, then any of three people could have done it—or perhaps all three or any combination. Barrett is the most likely, more so than Emily or Laura."

"Laura was just a kid at the time."

"Remember that story I told you about the grandmother, her cat and the two homicidal grandchildren?"

I made an appropriate noise to indicate it was not something I was likely to forget. "What's her motive, though?"

"Violet Francher's overbearing personality? One cannot choose one's relative."

"You could add a fourth, the housekeeper who quit."

"Ah, but she was very much elsewhere learning the duties of her job some ten miles away. On the other hand, that frayed wire could just as easily have been tampered with days earlier and left as a sort of waiting bomb, or the whole thing could have been an accident, after all."

"Look, is this anything we can really use?"

"It is knowledge, usable or not. Only time will reveal its value to us."

"So now what?"

Most of the green in his gills had faded and his eyes were sparking with new energy when he opened them. "We take a ride in a cab."

"We—you found the cab?"

"More important, I found the driver. His name is John Henry Banks and he is president, owner, and sole employee of Banks Cab Company. And"—he glanced at his watch—"he is due here in fifteen minutes."

"You talked with him?"

"I made an appointment by phone for him to pick us up."

"How in hell did you find him?"

"Sometimes in this type of work antic coincidence plays its part. One of the men I talked with today was part of the demolition and cleanup crew that worked on the burned Francher house. He mentioned that the day before they started the job, his cousin John Henry had been called out to the estate to pick up a fare. It should give you an idea of how exciting the pace of life is in Glenbriar that something so trivial is remembered."

"But it's a break for us."

"We shall see."

At seven-thirty a blue-and-yellow checkered cab pulled up outside the inn and a little brown man in gray work clothes and a peaked cap got out and stumped up to the front door.

"Call for Escott!" he bellowed, poking his head just inside.

I hoped Escott hadn't wanted a low profile for himself. If so, then John Henry Banks had just shot it all to hell. We'd already gotten a few curious looks from the desk clerk. Correction, I had gotten the looks. Escott had both our names on the register, but he'd been the only one they'd seen up till now. The clerk was giving me a fishy eye, trying to figure out where I'd come from.

We followed Banks out and Escott told him to drive to the edge of town. It took him all of one minute.

"Now where to?" he asked, looking at us from the rear-view mirror. I was squeezed flat against the door, but he got puzzled about the empty spot I should have been in and twisted around to make sure I was still aboard. Escott distracted him before things got out of hand.

"Mr. Banks, I have a question for you. . . ."

"Eh?"

"I need to know if you can recall a fare you picked up five years ago."

He gawked at us. He had a square face with a sharp nose and chin, thin brown hair, and large, innocent brown eyes. "You serious? Five years? I don't keep those kind of records, mister."

"Have you ever picked up a fare from the Francher estate?"

He started to roll his eyes and shake his head but stopped midway. "Here now, the Franchers'? The place where the old lady was burned up?"

"The same."

"I maybe could remember," he hazarded, his eyes flicking meaningfully to the running meter.

Escott smiled. "I'm sure you will, Mr. Banks, given the time. It's a fine cool night out and this country air is quite refreshing." He sat back in the seat as if it were part of a drawing room and he had all night to listen.

Banks responded with a grin. "Okay, as a matter of fact, I do remember that one."

"Please tell us about it."

"Why do you want to know?"

Escott now looked at the meter. "Then again, this air can be too much of a good thing. I shouldn't like to catch a chill, so perhaps we should return immediately to the inn. . . ."

Banks caught on fast. "Well, I was in my office—which is my house—and got his call. It's just me and the one car, you know, and business is pretty thin, so I'm open all the time. Anyway, this call comes telling me to come up to the Francher place, which I never been to before on account of the old lady and her daughter being rich with their own cars don't need any cabs. Course by then the old lady got burned up in the fire, my cousin Willie was gonna help tear down the old house—''

"The phone call, Mr. Banks?" Escott gently urged.

"Oh, yeah. I got out there, had to argue my way past Mayfair's wife—she's the housekeeper there, and what a temper she's got. You'd think she owned the place the way she throws her weight around. She went to call the house to see if anyone wanted a cab, and when she got back she looked like she'd just bit a bad lemon. Mayfair let me through and I drove up and saw the house—the burned one, and what a mess that was—''

Escott raised an eyebrow.

"Oh. Well. I got to the other house, the new place what the daughter had built, and there was this lady standing out front waiting—''

"What'd she look like?" I asked.

"I dunno. She was little, dark clothes, wore one of them hats so you couldn't see her face."

"With a veil?" Maureen often wore one to shade her eyes from the afterglow of sunset.

"Yeah. Looked like a widow at a funeral. She had a trunk, but I always keep some rope handy for stuff like that. It was some trouble I had trying to tie the thing in place—''

"Where did she want to go? What did she say to you?"

"She hardly said nothing, just told me to load the trunk on and to take her to Port Jefferson as quickly as I could."

"Where's that?"

"That's what threw me, too. I expected it to be at least to Queens, and this place is nearly sixty miles away in the opposite direction. It's along the north shore of the island. I asked if she was sure, and she nodded and got inside and told me to hurry it up.''

"She was nervous?"

"I guess so. She seemed plenty interested in getting going.''

"Was she afraid?"

"Dunno. Who could tell with that black stuff covering her face? All I can tell you for sure was that she was in a hurry.''

"Did she say why she was going to Port Jefferson?"

"I asked—by way of conversation, just to be friendly—but she never answered, so I shut up. Some of these rich dames can be pretty snooty. She was quiet for the whole trip, and sixty miles is a long way to be quiet.''

"Why did you think she was rich?" asked Escott.

"You think the Franchers would know anyone poor?" he reasoned logically.

"Where in Port Jefferson did you take her?"

"Now that's the funny part. She wanted to be dropped at the ferry.''

"Ferry?"

"Port Jefferson has a ferry running across the sound to Bridgeport. It was full night by then and the ferry was closed down and I told her so. She just had me untie her trunk and leave it there with her on the side of the road. She paid the fare, gave me a five-dollar tip, and I drove off feeling pretty good.''

"You seem to have a very clear memory of all this."

"I guess I do. I mean, besides this being the only person I ever picked up from the Francher place, she was the only person who ever gave me a tip that big. I ain't gonna forget something like that so soon.''

Escott turned to me. "What would she want in Bridgeport?"

I shrugged. Why would she want to be crossing water by boat? It was difficult enough for me to bear going over on a bridge.

He went back to John Henry Banks. "You are absolutely certain of this sequence of events?"

"That's the truth, mister. Take it or leave it."

He took it, but neither of us liked it.

Banks drove us back to the inn. It was my turn, so I paid off the meter and gave him a tip equal to Maureen's, which put him into an excellent mood. He grinned and thanked us along with instructions to call him anytime if we ever needed another drive.

Escott was striding purposefully up the stone-bordered walk. I caught up with him in the small lobby just as he was accepting a thin phone book from the desk clerk. I craned over his shoulder to see the pages.

He stopped at cab companies in the area—a very short listing—and Banks was at the top of the column, a fact Escott noted aloud to me.

"If she needed a taxi, she would consult a directory and the first listing might be her first choice, as it evidently turned out. How do you feel about a long drive tonight?"

"To Port Jefferson?"

"And possibly to Bridgeport."

On a boat. Across all that water. Damn.

"Or perhaps not," he added, noting my expression.

"I'm no Popeye the Sailor, but if Maureen could take it, so can I. I guess."

"Brave heart," he said, and signaled to the clerk to start checking us out.

While he was busy with that I went upstairs to bring down his bag and my trunk. I opened our door and stopped cold. Jonathan Barrett was standing by the window, hands clasped behind him and looking at me as though I, and not he, were the unwelcome intruder.

6

HE WAS BACK in twentieth-century clothing again, though a vestige of the past still clung to him with his ramrod posture and wind-combed hair. The five-second stare he gave me served as his only preamble. His eyes were cold, matching his tone of voice. "Last night I was made to understand that you were leaving for the city."

"We did." I quietly shut the door behind me. "And then we came back."

"Obviously. Why?"

"We had a little more checking to do."

"Yes, you've the dirty job of sifting through someone else's laundry. This is yet a dull village with gossip as the chief source of entertainment. It didn't take long for the story of your friend's pub crawling to filter back to our own servants' hall." He looked ready to belt me again and shoved down the impulse with a visible effort. "When *are* you planning to leave?"

"We're checking out now."

"For good?"

"Why are you so anxious about it?"

"I'm only protecting my—Miss Francher and her family. Having the two of you intruding into her private business is entirely abhorrent—"

"You mean about the fire?"

"Of course I do. What has it to do with your trying to find Maureen?"

"I thought maybe you could tell me."

"Tell me what? There's nothing to tell. The fire was over and done with long before Maureen ever came to see me."

"And you figure there's no connection?"

"How can there be?" He raised a hand. "No, don't bother answering that with another damned question. I can see you haven't the heart to care about the kind of damage you're doing."

"What damage?"

He started to shake his head in exasperation at my apparent stupidity, then caught on that I'd been trying to goad him.

"What damage, Barrett?" I pursued.

He said nothing and only glared.

"What are you afraid of?"

His face was hard now, nearly ugly from the emotions rumbling under the surface. He looked taller and I could almost feel the anger pulsing from him.

"If you were in my place, what would you be doing to find her?"

That one struck a chord. He paced the length of the small room once with slow steps, subsiding into himself. He stopped next to me, trying to bore a hole through my brain with his eyes. "You said you were checking out. Are you going for good?"

"I don't know."

"Why is that?"

"I can't really say."

"Because you lack knowledge or because you don't trust me?"

"You're sharp, Barrett."

"Yes, and I've had as much of you as I can stomach. Do what you must to find Maureen, but leave the Franchers out of it. Leave them alone and stay out of my way."

Or what? I asked him as much with my expression.

There was murder in his return look, and he took a step toward me to carry it out, or so I thought. The color abruptly faded from his dark clothes and his pale skin drained to the lifeless white of the truly dead. His outline wavered and swam in on itself, melting and merging into a shapeless, gray, man-sized *thing*.

Impossibly hanging in midair, it twisted like a slow cyclone and tore by me. The wake of its brushing passage pierced me to the bone with a rush of arctic cold. The gray mass slammed silently against the window panes, fell through them as though they weren't really there, and whirled away into the night wind. I rushed forward just in time to see it hurtle across the yard below to vanish into the cover of some intervening trees. A few moments later I heard the innocuous, ordinary roar of a car gunning to life. Its tires spun and screamed against the pavement, an audible expression of Barrett's anger.

Escott often complained that my disappearing act unnerved him. His limited human eyes missed most of the show, though. He didn't know about this, about what it looked like to me. I'd witnessed it once before myself, but not in the close, calm normality of a well-lighted room.

I was still shaking when he came upstairs to help with the luggage.

Sixty miles of bucolic country broken up by quaint towns and picturesque villages chock-full of historical significance can get to you after a while. An hour of it left me longing for the comfort of concrete, streetlights, and traffic signs. Barrett's visit had left a bad taste in my mind.

I'd told Escott all about it, of course. He listened but was inclined to shrug it off for the moment.

"The man has a point—" he started to say.

"But only if he's telling the truth about protecting the Franchers. It's more likely he's trying to protect himself. What I want to know is, what's he trying to hide?"

"Any number of things which we have discussed at length: his job, his regard for Miss Francher . . . and very possibly his condition."

"Condition? You mean—"

"Yes, the one you both share. That's a detail about yourself that you are wisely reluctant to reveal to people. I should imagine he feels the same way. An investigation such as ours could quickly place him in an untenable position. Would you not also be a bit nervous if someone started looking into your past and present?"

"Jeez, yes. But you said Violet Francher already tried to do that and it didn't faze him. So what's the difference now?"

"You, old man. You're the only one stopping him from fixing me with a basilisk gaze and instructing me to mind my own business. Perhaps he did do just that with Mrs. Francher's own agent. This time he is denied the luxury and is no doubt suffering from the frustration of it all."

He was right, but I was still uneasy and promised myself to keep both eyes wide open if we went back to Glenbriar. I was safe enough, but if Barrett lost his temper, he could snap Escott like a twig—body or mind, take your pick.

Escott helped to make the rest of the trip bearable by reporting on his day and the other details he'd discovered about the Francher household.

"The maid, cook, housekeeper, and gardener are all employees of long standing with Miss Emily. When Barrett arrived, some horses were acquired, along with a groom to care for them. Barrett is the only employee to actually sleep in the house now. When the maid and cook were moved out to live over the garage, the natural conclusion was that they were not meant to see certain things, hence the gossip."

"Which has some truth behind it, from what I saw the other night," I put in.

He acknowledged with a nod. "Yes, though I may also add that there is a general sympathy for their employer because of the way her mother died. Few people seem ready to condemn the woman for keeping a handsome young man on the payroll.''

''What do these people think of Barrett?''

''I can only report that hardly anyone outside the immediate household has ever seen him; which has also garnered the general approval of the locals. If there is something 'going on,' he has the good manners to confine himself to the Francher estate and is not attempting to spread his wicked ways among his neighbors.''

''Does that include any society people?''

''Miss Francher has willfully cut herself off from her social and financial peers, so they are relieved of the unpleasant duty of making any public judgment of her private life. That Miss Francher is excluded from their tea parties and other events of import matters not one whit to the lady.''

''And her family?''

''That is something I plan to check into—but discreetly,'' he added, catching my look. ''I have no wish to call the wrath of Mr. Barrett down upon my head.''

''Amen.''

''As for the inhabitants of Glenbriar, Emily Francher may do whatever she pleases in private, as long as it stays that way. If she were anyone else, she'd find life a bit more hostile.''

''The old Hester Prynne bit?''

Not having the benefit of an American education, he didn't understand the reference. I gave him a brief summary of Hawthorne's book until he did.

He agreed with the general idea, but added one of his own. ''Perhaps it is closer to the point to say that her money makes the difference here. If a poor man does something out of the norm, he's condemned for a lunatic. When a rich man indulges in kind, he is affectionately tolerated as an eccentric. Thus we have it that no one thinks anything strange about the very late hours kept by the principals of the household.''

"They're a pretty understanding bunch around here."

"The Francher bills are always paid on time. That counts for much in terms of tolerance and goodwill these days."

"These days more than most."

Conversation lagged for a quarter hour and I watched the woods on either side blur past.

"Sixty miles is a long way to be quiet," Escott quoted, breaking the silence by doing a perfect mimic of Banks. It jolted me, kicking a vagueness into a certainty.

"It's too much."

"What is?"

"The tip. Banks said he got a five-dollar tip from Maureen. It's too much."

"Perhaps she thought it to be a necessary compensation after such a long trip."

"No, think about her past, about the time she grew up in. In those days you tipped in pennies."

"Some women eschew the practice altogether."

"She wasn't one of them. I mean, she did all right for herself, but she was never one to throw her money around. In an extravagant mood she might have tipped him a buck, but never five, not unless she pulled the wrong bill out by mistake."

"That could well have been the case."

"Yeah." But I still had some doubt souring my mind and he knew it.

"What alternative do you suggest?" he asked.

"Like maybe five years ago Barrett called Banks out to the house and put it into his head he was taking Maureen to Port Jefferson. He gave him the fare and a five-dollar tip to help him remember it all the way he's supposed to."

"Complicated. Why should he do that?"

"So it looks on the level with Mayfair or anyone else who might have seen her arrive at the estate."

"Such as Emily Francher?"

"Well, figure it. Barrett's got a soft spot for himself with her, and then Maureen shows up. She doesn't like what he's doing and could queer it for him but good if she drops the wrong word in Emily's ear.''

"Would she have done so?''

"That doesn't matter. What does is that Barrett thought she would.''

"And you think Barrett—''

"Might have done something. Yeah.''

"That he might have killed Maureen?''

After a long time I said, "Yeah,'' and I hated saying it.

Port Jefferson had a shipyard, some gravel pits, and the ferry, all dark now. Compared to Glenbriar it was a bustling metropolis, which wasn't saying much, but then some places aren't at their best at night. Escott and I split up. I took the hotels and he went to inflict more damage on his liver at the taverns. I advised him to find a diner first and line his stomach with the biggest, greasiest butter-fried hamburger he could handle. He didn't look thrilled at the prospect, but nodded agreement and walked off with a grim set to his jaw.

Maureen's stopover—if she had stopped—had taken place at the height of the tourist season. No one remembered a lone woman with a trunk arriving at night five years ago. I talked my way into examining hotel-registration books and learned a lot about kindness from various clerks and managers offering what help they could.

After running out of hotels, I checked out all the boardinghouses I could find, even knowing that Maureen would have avoided them as a matter of course. Like me, she would have preferred the relative privacy and anonymity of a hotel to spend her vulnerable daylight time. But I had to be certain. I covered everything.

Hours later, options exhausted, I climbed back into the car to wait for Escott. We had no set time to meet, though. When the first faint pangs of hunger started up I went in search of a meal.

No stockyards and no stables; it looked like the locals only ate fish, and duck—at least in the business district. I widened my hunting radius to less urbanized areas and soon caught the unmistakable scent of cow manure on a random puff of wind.

There were more stops than starts involved following it, but my nose eventually led me to an open field populated by several bovines clustered under a tree. I climbed through the fence, watched where my feet were going, and strolled up.

They seemed to know I wasn't there for an old-fashioned milking. As a cow, they all moved away. Picking one out, I optimistically followed. She proved to be quite agile for her size and energetic after spending the whole day eating her head off. Though country bred myself, I'd forgotten how fast cattle can move when they want to, and my dinner got away.

I picked out another, waited until it stopped, and calculated the distance. It bawled unhappily as though reading my mind. Disappearing, I rushed forward, felt its bulk loom close, and went solid with my arms reaching out to wrap around its neck.

The cow had other ideas and bawled again, tossing herself (and me) around like a rodeo trainee. She dragged me over half the field, deaf to my urgent pleas for quiet and oblivious to that special influence I usually have over animals. It only belatedly occurred to me that all the other animals had been in small pens with no place to run. I let go, managed to stay on my soggy feet, and old Bossy galloped off to be with the rest of the girls.

It was ridiculous. I had an easier job finding cooperative livestock in the heart of the city. After a few feet of weary trudging, I noticed the disgusting state of my shoes and opted to go transparent the rest of the way. The wind was in the right direction; I let it take me toward a group of buildings at the far end of the field.

By now I had trouble telling the difference between the yard manure and the supply I had with me. Each shed had to be examined by sight, not smell. Unfortunately, it is also almost impossible to take a casual walk through a working farm. You not only have to contend with uneven and odorous ground clutter and mud, but the local tenants as well. Never mind Farmer Jones and his shotgun, it's his animals that are dangerous.

Chickens are fairly brainless and confined to coops, but ducks are usually allowed to roam free to scavenge and play in their pond. It was just my bad luck that I blundered right into a flock and sent them on a panicky flight to safety. Mixed in with them were a few geese who made more commotion than all the rest together. In turn, they alerted a small pack of large dogs who charged in helter-skelter, baying in full voice. Their owner coming out of the house packing a gun with a double load of buckshot was a mere afterthought. I didn't stick around to see how the show came out, but vanished and shot up in the general direction of the main barn.

My amorphous form bounced unexpectedly against the vertical wall of wood, nearly sending me solid with the shock. I clung there against the wind and frantically felt around for an opening into the hayloft. It was just above me; I thankfully dribbled over the edge to re-form—and nearly rolled right off my perch. Instead of the loft, I'd shot too high and was hanging onto the roof, and oh, God, I hate heights.

Far, far below, Old MacDonald was circling the yard stirring up the geese and giving a lot of unexpected fun to his pack of semi-tame, lop-eared wolves. They were tearing all over the place, heads down and tails happily fanning, eager to show master how good they were at their job. So what if they never found a thing and only ended up anointing every likely projection turn in turn? It was a great break in the routine.

Shutting my eyes against the dizzy drop, I vanished again and seeped through the barn roof, inching down until I came in contact with a horizontal surface. A second later I ascertained that it was the straw-littered floor of the loft and fairly safe. I lay flat and rested body and mind until the circus outside finally died away.

The barn wasn't much different from the one I'd played in as a kid. I was aware of chickens and mice and another, much larger animal somewhere below. I could have used a ladder, but didn't want to risk making more noise and rousing the dogs again. Far better to disappear and float down to the safe, sane ground.

It was closed up against the night, but seeing in the dark was no problem for me. Over in one partitioned-off corner was a drab white draft horse only a little smaller than Escott's Nash. He was the four-legged answer to a hungry vampire's prayer, and I trotted toward him as though greeting a long-lost friend.

And stopped.

He moved restlessly, his head low and with his ears flat along the skull. His near-hind hoof was raised a little, all set to kick me into the next state as soon as I got in range. If his vocal cords had been designed for it, he'd have been growling.

It just wasn't my night.

Escott was in the car and taking a short snooze. He woke with a slight start when I crawled into the passanger side and flopped wearily back in the seat. My fatigue was mental, not physical.

"Good heavens, where have you been?" he asked, his long nose wrinkling.

"E-i-e-i-o," I muttered darkly, daring him to comment. He read the signs right and restrained himself.

It had been a struggle, but I finally persuaded Dobbin to part with some of what he obviously had too much of. He was a reluctant bastard and considered me to be no better than your average trespasser and thief. When finished, I made a fast and invisible exit from his stall, very mindful of his huge hooves. There was no point giving him a pat of thanks, he'd have only tried to take my arm off at the roots.

Escott had also been drinking, but was showing less wear and tear. As before, he had only a slight glaze to his eyes to indicate he was in no pain.

"You learn anything?" I asked.

He shook his head. "Did you?"

I shook my head.

"Care to go to Bridgeport?" he asked.

During his alcoholic rambles, Escott encountered a man with a boat who was ready to take us across the sound no matter what the hour. He'd had no similar requests five years ago from a lone lady and didn't know of anyone else who had. For a fee, the low, fast launch left over from his days as a rum runner was at our command.

I grimaced at the wide sweep of Long Island Sound. It was silver and calm under the steel-colored sky, a beautiful enough sight from the land. I hadn't always been afraid of water and could still slosh around in a bathtub with the best, but since my change, huge bodies of the open, free-flowing kind sent me into the sick miseries.

"I think I'd like to sit this one out," I finally answered.

"Really?" he asked, in a tone that wanted to know why.

Maybe it had to do with my basic need to be in contact with the earth, or maybe it's because I'd been murdered over water. I'd had some recent and very bad experiences occurring in or near water. Driving over it on a bridge was one thing, but crossing all of that bleak expanse in a tiny boat was quite another. I was hard put to suppress an involuntary shudder at the thought of only a thin shell of wood holding back such endless, smothering cold.

I tried to give him an explanation that made sense, but he waved me down after the first few stumbling words.

"That's all right," he said. "I understand."

"I'm not running out on you, am I?"

"No." He sounded fairly amused. "Of course you aren't.

I know it's not easy for you at times—and I find that strangely reassuring.''

I waved once at him from the shore as the launch started to cut its way across the sound. He was looking back, but didn't respond. Not having my night vision, he couldn't see me. With an inward smile, I got back in the car and drove off to one of the better hotels I'd found earlier that evening.

After some personal cleanup, I padded downstairs to find someone brave enough to scrape my shoes back to respectability again. The lobby was as deserted as a church on Saturday night. This was no city hotel with twenty-four-hour clerks to keep you company. The man who'd checked me in had worn his slippers, bathrobe, and a sleepy, resigned expression.

Not dressed for a walk, I was too restless to just sit in my room with the radio on. I was at a loss for activity until I spotted the pay phone. A whole pocketful of change was going to waste in my pants; I fished it all out and got an operator on the line.

Bobbi answered on the first ring and we exclaimed our hellos and ''I miss yous'' for a while, and she assured me she'd been awake, reminding me there was still a time difference between Chicago and New York.

''New York is old news,'' I told her. ''We're on Long Island now.''

''Why? You taking some kind of scenic route?''

''We're following up a lead.''

''A good one?''

''Doesn't look it, but Charles wants to be thorough.''

''What got you up there?''

''This and that. We . . . we turned up Maureen's old boyfriend.''

There was a long pause on her end. ''He's like you?''

''Yeah.''

''How like you? I mean, what's he like?''

"Well, he's no Dracula, if that's what you're worried about."

"I was, a little."

"If anything, he's sort of a cross between a lounge lizard and Captain Blood."

"Captain *who*?"

Considering my dietary habits, it'd been an alarming reference to bring up. I quickly explained about Sabatini's pirate-hero.

"You don't like him much," she deduced, meaning Barrett and not Sabatini.

"It's mutual, believe me. He's all manners, but I'm watching my back."

"Then why would Maureen have gotten involved with him?"

That question had been eating at me as well. "He's just the type, I guess."

"What type is that?"

"The type who always has women stampeding to get to him. Right now it looks like he'll be stringing two of them along at once."

"Sleeping with both of them?" she asked, always one for clarity.

"It's heading that way—and try this on: they all live in the same house. One of them has money and the other's all ready to seduce him."

"Then he's some kind of a twenty-four-carat idiot," she sniffed. "The same house? That's just asking for trouble. Sooner or later his meal ticket'll figure things out. You can't keep news like that from a woman—we're naturally suspicious."

"You suspicious about me?"

"Of course not, I know you'll never meet anyone else who's better in bed with you than I am."

"You've got me spoiled rotten, sweetheart," I agreed.

And we steamed up the lines with similar talk until an

operator broke in to say our time was up and did we want another three minutes? She must have been listening in; I could almost see the smirk on her face that her voice suggested. I dropped in more money and ignored her.

"Listen, Bobbi, I want to ask you something."

"You know the answer to that is yes."

"Thanks, but it'll have to wait until I'm back."

"Damn," she said cheerfully.

"I just wondered, would you ever tip a cab driver five bucks?"

She was shocked. "Five bucks? You think I'm one of the Carnegies or something?"

"Would you ever?"

"Only if I were delirious and lost on the South Side in a sleet storm on Christmas Eve."

"So what kind of woman tips a cabbie five bucks?"

"One that doesn't know what it's worth. You're talking about the idle rich, honey—someone who never had to work for it."

"That's what I thought."

"What's this got to do with things?"

"I'll find that out tomorrow night."

"So when are you coming back?"

"I don't know, baby. Expect me when you see me."

She made a rude noise to communicate her disappointment. "Then get yourself a raincoat. The papers say there's a hurricane moving up the coast and headed your way. I don't want you catching cold from all that wet."

I wasn't certain I could still catch a cold, but took the sentiment as it was given, promising to bundle up for her sake. We said good-bye until the operator cut in again, and then hung up.

The rest of the night went by like paint drying, though I spent some of it scribbling out a note to Escott about Bobbi's views on tipping. I didn't know how useful it would be, but thought it worth pointing out again. After his return I planned to make another visit to the Francher estate, with or without Barrett's permission.

I experienced déjà vu waking up in the Glenbriar Inn again. My trunk was in the same place as before, but pulled out far enough from the wall so I could lift the lid. Escott was there this time, stretched out on his bed, and contentedly up to his neck in newsprint, past and present.

"So what happened in Bridgeport?" I asked, when my few seconds of confusion passed.

"Nothing, as you may have gathered by our return here. I went to taxi companies and examined police, hospital, and as many hotel records as I could manage. I checked morgue records for Jane Does . . ."

He got a sharp look from me.

". . . as a matter of course. She might have thought to use an alias, so I searched for Barretts, Flemings, and Franchers as well as Does and Dumonts. There is no official indication she stopped at all in Bridgeport. She may have merely passed through it, but then one could say there is no real evidence she ever crossed the sound in the first place."

All that footwork and probably a hangover to boot, no wonder he looked stretched and discouraged. "What'd you think of my note?" I'd left it on top of my trunk in Port Jefferson for him to find.

Now he smiled thinly. "We have returned, have we not? I'm strongly inclined to agree with the insights the two of you have concerning that excessive tip. All our roads appear to lead back to the Franchers. A new beginning is in order and we need to start with them."

"That's what I wanted. I'm going out to the house again tonight to see if I can fix up a private little talk with Emily. You have to figure she must know something. Unless Barrett got one of the maids to impersonate Maureen, Emily's just right for the part."

"What about Laura?"

"Too tall. Maureen and Emily are about the same height and build."

"Excellent point."

"You get any more from the locals today?" I noticed that a general lassitude permeated his manner and movements and guessed that he'd been working his butt off in one of the taverns again.

"Most of the talk was about a hurricane that's been coming up the coast. The papers are forecasting massive death and destruction to arrive here soon, and people are busy tying things down in preparation. There's already been a little rain."

I groaned inside. Not so many nights ago, I'd had enough rain to last a few lifetimes; much more and I'd be tempted to move to Death Valley.

"Perhaps you should wait until it blows over," he suggested.

"Nah, I'm all ready to go do it now. I'll go crazy if I have to sit around a hotel room another night memorizing the wallpaper."

"I see your point."

"Look, Charles, this could take a lot of time. Did you really feel like coming along just to wait out in a damp car?"

"Put that way, it does sound most unappealing."

"Besides, you did all that work today; it's my turn now."

He surrendered without argument. "By all means go on without me. I could certainly use a quiet evening of rest."

Lightly put, but he was tired, and I felt better for having him safe at the Glenbriar—away from Barrett and any unforeseen problems.

I wore a dark shirt and black pants with my raincoat. The few tourists hanging around the lobby gaped at me as if I were an out-of-place mobster. They quickly huddled back into their mah-jongg game to resume discussion about how run down things were becoming with that Democrat in the White House.

The rented Ford was in a gravel lot behind the inn. I braved a stiff breeze and a few thick drops of rain and nosed it onto the road.

The possibility of Barrett discovering me going about my unlawful trespass of his employer's property kept my mind unpleasantly busy. Not that illegal entry was something to weigh on my conscience; I was simply shrinking from the embarrassment of getting caught. I planned to be very, very careful.

Preoccupied with the evening ahead, I took a wrong turn and found myself going in a miles-wide circle back to Glenbriar. The rain was coming down heavily and the wind gusted against the car, rocking it. I couldn't go back, the road was too narrow for a U-turn, and I didn't want to chance getting stuck in one of the steep ditches running along either side of the paving. I squinted ahead for a crossroad or driveway to use.

A mile later, the rain was pouring so hard that I was going less than half the posted speed limit. The wind drove the water straight at the front window, making the wipers useless. The headlights only bounced off a shimmering quicksilver wall, illuminating nothing. My night vision was no good for this kind of a mess. The speedometer pointer dropped down below ten miles an hour and I still felt I was going too fast.

Escott had had the right idea about a quiet evening resting up. It was past time to call it a night. At this point I wasn't all that sure of finding my way back to Glenbriar, much less getting to the Francher estate. Even if I did reach it, I was facing a long walk through the woods, and I could hardly conceal my presence while leaving a dripping trail throughout the house. Unless the hurricane blew it into the sound, the place would still be there tomorrow.

Its taillights were on—the only warning I had of its presence. I hit the brakes, skidded badly, but stopped just short of back-ending a car stopped in the road. I punched my horn once. They didn't move. Disgusted, I decided to pull around and hoped no one was coming up in the other lane to hit me.

A semi-clear patch opened in the shifting gray curtain of water. My headlights just caught the bright blue-and-yellow check design on the trunk of the car.

Glenbriar was only a small town and John Henry Banks was someone I'd be bound to run into again before our business was ended, but I suddenly got very cold inside. The uneasy feeling persisted the longer I sat and thought about it, getting worse instead of better as I tried to come up with a good reason for Banks to be out here tonight. Scowling at the rain, I swallowed back my fears and levered out of the car into the hurricane.

It was like standing under Niagara, except the water was horizontal instead of vertical because of the wind. I put my back to it, steadied myself with a hand on the car, and staggered over to the passenger door of the cab. It was on the lee side and offered some minuscule protection against the raw force trying to bowl me over.

I couldn't see inside the window for all of the water streaming down. I thumped on the door a few times on the off chance that I was interrupting a lovers' rendezvous and opened it.

As it turned out, I wasn't interrupting anything. It was all finished by now.

Banks was heeled over on his right side, one arm curled beneath him and the other trailing off under the dashboard. His eyes sagged open, looking at nothing. His pockets were turned out and a few stray coins littered the floor. Blood covered his head and face and flooded the seat where he lay. The red smell of it smothered my senses and jammed all thought.

Maybe I said something. I don't know. The shock had hit like a block of ice, leaving me stunned. As though someone else were doing it for me, my hand went out in a futile effort to find a pulse.

"Cha . . ."

I jumped like I'd touched a hot wire. Banks was alive.

". . . nged." Nonsense slurred from his slack mouth. His eyes were still open and fixed. He was unaware of me.

I leaned in close. "Banks, who did it?"

"Change," he said clearly.

Disturbed by me, a quarter dropped from the edge of the seat and hit the floor. The sound as it landed was lost, masked over by the storm.

"Who hit you, Banks? Who did it?"

"Not."

"Who was it? Did you know him?"

"Lie."

I didn't dare move him. I needed help, but didn't know where to go to find it. A house with a phone could be only yards away, but invisible in the rain. Maybe I could flag down another car if it passed by.

"Was it a man? A woman?"

"Tall."

"Who, Banks?"

"F-fine."

"Banks!"

His eyes were still open, but he'd slipped away. My hand was touching his neck and I felt it happen. The knowledge spread up from my fingers straight to the brain and coiled down my spine. One second he was a man with dreams and needs and desires like the rest of us, and the next he was an inert, empty carcass.

A slow and sticky kind of sickness started in my guts and began working its way up. I quickly backed out of the cab, holding on to the door for support, and sucked in drafts of cold air and rain. I did not vomit in the ditch running along the roadside, though it would have been a kind of release. My condition doesn't always allow me the luxury of a human weakness. The bile stayed in my throat, clinging to the back of my mouth, and wouldn't go away.

I checked Banks. He was dead, I'd not made a mistake. The side of his head was smashed in, hard. The killer had been very fast; so fast that Banks had had no time to blink. I reached in and closed his eyes with numb fingers.

The bile surged inside. Maybe I was going to be sick, after all. I backed out again, the rain whirling around me, and leaned on the cab for support.

I heard a close, sharp *thud*.

My feet slipped away from under me. I toppled forward against the cab, cracking my chin hard on the wet roof.

Thud.

I felt the second blow and sprawled flat on my face on the streaming road. Water bounced up from the paving, stinging and filling my eyes.

The third was much harder. My head was firmly braced against the unyielding road surface. Whoever was doing it could bring a lot of momentum to bear with their downward swing.

The fourth.

I couldn't hear the rain hissing anymore. The world was reduced to cottony silence and the softly pulsing light beneath my eyelids.

The fifth.

The light was gone.

I don't remember the sixth or seventh.

Just as well.

7

Rain pelting against my sodden coat.

Light.

A hand on my wrist.

Mitch, are they—

My God, Elma, get back in the car. Fear in his voice.

Footsteps. A door slams shut.

The man keeps saying *my God* over and over again before he finally backs away and leaves.

His voice raises in a shout, then a curse.

The wet rush and roar as a car drives quickly past.

Rain.

Wind.

Another car. The road under me announces its approach.

He shouts again. This time it stops. Light pierces my sightless eyes. Voices.

. . . get to a phone . . .

. . . Trent place, just up the road . . .

. . . police first, it's too late for . . .

More lights, more voices. Questions.

An eternity of rain and wind.

. . . thought something was wrong so we stopped . . .

. . . Johnnie Banks, don't know who the other fella . . .

Hands probe my pockets.

. . . out of town. Must be his car behind Johnnie's . . .

The light gets stronger. It beats on me like the rain. Hands turn my body. Rain strikes my face.

. . . cracked open like an egg . . .

Want to scream. Can't.

. . . multiple blows with a blunt instrument, both of 'em. That's as much as I can tell . . .

. . . musta been a robbery, but who . . .

Hands on my body, lifting me.

The rain stops. Full daylight. Blinding, burning, killing daylight.

Want to scream. Want to scream.

They drop a blanket on me. The rough fabric covers my face. Grunting and swaying, they carry my body out of the wind.

The blanket diffuses the light a little.

Can't move or talk.

A car rumbles under me.

Hands and movement. Hands tugging, pulling at me, at my clothes. No way to tell them to stop.

Searing white light cuts into my brain. Cold air on my bare skin. Icy water sluices over me. Nose and mouth clog with it. They turn my head. The water drains away.

Hands probe my broken skull.

Can't scream.

. . . we'd like to respect it, but in the case of a homicide, we have to have the doctor . . .

Arguments drift over me. One voice is vaguely familiar.

Someone closes my light-blind eyes. Red and black patches drift under the lids.

. . . notify his family . . .

. . . working for me, it's my job to . . .

The voices fade. They throw a heavy sheet on me. Out of sight. Out of mind.

The sun works free of the clouds. It beats silently against the covering.

Someone lifts the sheet. The sun flashes over me like a

furnace. Something is shoved under me, firmly pushed under the small of my back.

It's the peace of the grave.

Out. Out. Out.

Sweet night.

A voice. A question.

And pain. Far too much pain.

". . . hear me? Jack?"

My head feels like a bomb crater. If I lie very, very still, it might not get worse.

The voice whispers anxiously.

I remember the rain and the road and yes, I can hear you, so shut up.

A hand touches my bare shoulder. He tries shaking me awake. It moves my head. I scream. It comes out as little more than a bubbling exhalation.

"Jack?"

Dear God, stop the pain.

"Can you hear me?"

More bubbles. The taste of mud.

"Jack?"

A series of small coughs. Someone whimpers.

The questions stop. He carefully turns my head to the left. It eases the pressure on the cracked and broken plates of bone. He's as gentle as possible.

It's too much.

Out.

A clock ticking. A heart beating. Both are nearby.

"Jack?"

The pain had subsided a fraction. This was heaven by comparison.

"Can you hear me?"

Leave me alone.

"Can you understand me?"

Yeah, now go away for a few weeks.

"Please answer me, Jack."

I inhaled to speak, but couldn't get the mouth to work.

"What's my name?"

If you don't know, you're in worse trouble than I am.

"Answer me."

Inhalation. "Charl . . ."

A long sigh of relief. Not from me. He'd been afraid. Of what?

"Do you know what happened to you?"

"Road . . . rain."

"Yes, you were driving."

And then I stopped. An accident?

"You found the taxi," he prompted.

John Henry Banks. Johnnie Banks. Slumped over, mumbling nonsense. His head smashed in . . . no more, I don't want to think.

"Do you know who did it?"

God, was that me asking Banks or Escott asking me? I really couldn't tell.

"Did you see them?"

"Hurt. I hurt."

"I know. Do you need blood?"

I needed something, like an aspirin the size of a boxcar. "Try."

He put a thin rubber tube to my lips like a straw. I drew the stuff in. It was no longer warm from being in the animal, but still wonderful. The blood spread through me with its promise of life and healing, and then I didn't think about anything until it was gone.

"Better?" he asked, his voice faint.

"A little."

He pulled the tube away and ran some water, cleaning up. He liked to have things clean and neat. The water stopped.

"Can you open your eyes?"

Why not? The darkness seeped away for an instant. Escott's worried face hovered close to my own and was gone.

"Did you see anything?" he asked.

"Yeah. Fine."

F-fine. The last thing Banks had said and then—

"Try it again."

I did. They stayed open a few seconds longer. "Okay?"

"Excellent. They're a nice healthy red."

The white-hot hammer and anvil on the side of my skull wasn't pounding quite so hard.

"Think you'll be able to travel soon?"

He had to be out of his mind. I didn't want to move for a month.

"I have to get you out of here before morning."

You'd better have a damn good reason. "No. Rest."

"Yes, at least for now. Do you know who did it?"

That question again. "Banks knew. They get me?"

"You were struck from behind. The doctor found wood splinters in your scalp."

Multiple blows from a blunt instrument. The phrase repeated through my brain like an echo from a dream. Wood. Deadly, deadly wood. No wonder I was so helpless. "How bad?"

"You've a hell of a fracture, they hit you several times. I was worried you might not be—did you see them at all?"

"No."

I noticed the general darkness, or rather the absence of artificial light for the first time. He was also keeping his voice low, almost to a whisper. Faint outside illumination came from a high, uncurtained window. The dimness turned his skin ghost white and simplified his features.

As I drew air to speak, the smell crashed in: formaldehyde mixed with the sweetness of old death. A chill shuddered all through me that had nothing to do with the cold air.

"Where?"

"I'm afraid we're at the local funeral parlor," he explained, as though embarrassed by the fact. ''It doubles as the coroner's examination room in the case of questionable deaths or homicides.''

''Deaths?''

''I'll go into details when you've rested. You're much better than you were, much better than I'd hoped. After that fresh blood has had a chance to work in you we'll see about getting you out.''

''Out?''

''My position with the local authorities is anything but cordial, and I've no wish to be arrested for body snatching. It will be much easier for both of us if the body in question is able to move out under its own power.''

The meaning and import began to sink in. Instead of a bed, I was on a high metal table wearing only an old sheet. ''I'm dead—I mean, more so than usual?''

''As far as the law is concerned, yes.''

I had a nightmare flash in my head of a sealed coffin with muddy earth being heaped on top.

''Not yet.'' He'd stopped me from moving. ''We've time— almost the whole night, if you need it.'' He found a chair and sat down to wait.

Well, if he was in no hurry, neither was I. I rested and felt my battered head ache and listened to the clock tick. For something to do, I counted the ticks, getting up to thirty before losing track. This went on for as many times as I had fingers since I curled one up whenever I lost the count. When I'd twice made fists, I tried a little movement. My arms worked, the legs responded, but the head wasn't ready to coordinate anything more complicated than that.

The clock ticked and Escott breathed, and one by one, I curled my fingers. It was something I used to do to trick myself to sleep on bad nights. Sleep would have been a better way to pass the time, but I no longer really slept. I missed it.

After an hour, I managed to get my legs off the table and

was trying to push myself upright. My head was impossibly heavy. Escott got up to help.

"Shoulders only," I told him.

"Right."

Supporting the base of my neck, he helped boost me to a sitting position. I wobbled dizzily like a baby, but didn't fall. The sheet slipped down a little and I wrinkled my nose in disgust.

"Christ, don't they ever wash this stuff?"

He took my complaining as a good sign. "I've some fresh clothes for you. The ones you were found in are a bit of a write-off."

"My wallet?"

"The police have your personal effects." He produced a sack, pulling out some pants, a clean shirt, and some slippers.

"My shoes?" I'd brought only one pair.

"They're locked in that room over there." He nodded at a closed door.

"How'd you get in?"

"Through a rear window with a glass cutter," he said casually.

The dizziness from sitting up gradually passed. I felt the back of my head with supreme care—even my hair hurt. It was still fiery and tender, but the hammer and anvil had finally stopped pounding.

"What'd they do to me here?" I was remembering the not-so-gentle probing hands on my scalp.

"You were given a preliminary exam on the scene and pronounced dead, then they brought you here for—" He stopped.

"Jesus, Charles, an autopsy?"

He could only nod, looking as queasy as I felt.

The doctor'd make a fast Y-incision and scatter pieces of me over the counters in jars full of preservative. Dear God.

My arms wrapped tightly around my chest and stomach in reaction.

"What stopped them?"

"I did. I said I had to notify your family first, and then I told them you were a Christian Scientist."

My jaw dropped of its own accord, as it usually does when I don't understand something. "Huh?"

"I said they were like orthodox Jews in that their religion absolutely forbade autopsies."

"Does it?"

He suddenly smiled. "Actually, I haven't the least idea, but it worked for the time being, and that's all that matters."

"Why didn't you say I was an orthodox Jew?"

"I could not because you were out driving round after sunset on a Friday, the beginning of their Sabbath; something a practicing Jew would have avoided." He offered me the shirt.

I slowly dragged it on. It was clean and crisp with starch, but I still felt soiled. I wanted a scalding hot tub and a long vacation—in that order. He steadied me as I slid off the table to pull the pants up over my rump.

"We still staying at the inn?"

"Officially, *I* am. We'll just have to sneak you in somehow."

"They think—"

"You're dead. Yes, I've received much sympathy, at least in some quarters."

"What d'ya mean?"

"The police have told me not to leave town for the moment. They're probably strapped for suspects. It was fortunate for me that I was down in the lobby listening to the radio with some of the other guests during the critical time the crime took place or I would be in a very awkward position."

"Why should they suspect you?"

"Why not? Many people are murdered by their friends."

"And Banks?"

"I'm a stranger in town and Mr. Banks mentioned us to a few of his drinking cronies." His head went down and he leaned tiredly against a counter. "I should have been more careful. All my questions concerning the Franchers and that fire . . . I blundered badly and poor Banks paid for it."

"It might not even be connected to us."

"Can you believe that?"

I didn't answer that one. "You couldn't have known what would happen."

He shook his head, not really listening. "I am very much to blame for this, Jack. The police are not far off in their suspicions. The investigating officer is no fool, he knows I'm not telling him everything."

"And you can't, can you?"

"Not so that I would be believed and not without solid evidence. If Barrett is behind this, we need proof, and if we obtain proof, how may he be brought to justice?"

"If?"

"I am as yet uncertain of his guilt."

"After all this? Why?"

"I shall be glad to tell you, but elsewhere, if you please. Preferably at the inn so I can establish an alibi for part of this night. When they come in tomorrow and miss you, I shall certainly have to face some questioning. My strong objections to the autopsy will not have been forgotten in so short a time."

"What'll you do?"

"My best performance of moral outrage—after they inform me of the abduction of my poor friend's remains."

"Couldn't I just show up and say it was all a mistake and claim catalepsy or something?"

He shot me a look.

"No, I guess not."

"Do you feel ready to go?"

"After I get my shoes back."

"Perhaps you shouldn't. They're bound to notice."

"You think they'll worry about a pair of shoes when the whole body takes a walk?"

He couldn't argue with that one and nodded.

If I took things slowly, I could move. At the locked door, I leaned against it and seeped right through without even trying hard, which was a surprise. It took a lot more effort and concentration to solidify, though. Dematerialized, there was no discomfort, but I was reluctant to stay that way out of a sneaking fear of not being able to come back again. My head was tender inside and out and I wasn't planning to do anything fancy for a while.

The adjoining room was an office with wooden cabinets and functional furniture. My muddy, wrinkled clothes were scattered over a long table along with Banks's blood-spattered garments. Feeling sick and sad, I made myself look at them and remembered him.

I grabbed up my shoes, took off the evidence tag, and slipped them on. When I returned to the other room, Escott was just putting away a length of rubber tubing and a quart-size milk bottle.

"Is that what blood comes in these days?" I asked.

"It does when I collect it."

"How'd you get it this time?"

"I looked for and found a likely farm late this afternoon. If you were to recover—and I'm very glad you have—it seemed logical to provide for it. Blood appears to be the universal panacea for all your ills, and I wanted to be prepared."

"Thanks."

He shrugged it off, not one for gushing gratitude. It only embarrassed him.

"What'd you tell the farmer, that you were making blood sausage?"

"No, but that is a good suggestion. I said I was collecting blood samples from some of the area livestock."

"Didn't he think it kind of strange?"

"Yes, but fortunately the fellow was a Democrat, and that helped. I said I was a veterinarian working for the NRA and our branch of it was researching blood ailments in cattle. We needed samples for testing and offered monetary compensation for each pint collected."

"Sounds crazy to me."

"He must have thought so as well, but as they say, money talks. I got the samples."

"I'm glad."

"Well, you did buy me dinner the other night. . . ." He turned back to the table I'd spent the day on and swept up a small dark packet and shoved it into his bag.

"What's that?"

"A sample of your home soil. I managed to sneak it in under you when no one was looking."

"You think of everything."

"Not always," he muttered, and I knew he was mulling over Banks's death.

He climbed onto a counter next to the wall and pushed open the window above it. The way was clear and he wriggled through. I wasn't up to such exertions and did my usual vanishing act, reappearing at his side, but staggering a little. I'd had to fight to come back again, and it was draining. He caught my arm and led me away.

"It's a bit of a walk," he said. "They impounded the car as evidence."

"How far?"

"About a half mile. Can you make it?"

"I'll have to." I kept my groans to myself. I hurt, but was recovering incredibly fast. I'd been damned lucky.

We didn't talk and I concentrated on putting one foot in front of another. The air was clean and cool, inviting me to indulge in a bout of breathing. It quickly flushed the taste of the mortuary from my lungs.

Escott followed a less direct route to the Glenbriar Inn, taking a back street running parallel to the main road. It was a longer, more discreet walk, but after five minutes, witnesses to his night raid were the least of our worries.

We were about to cross an intersection when I chanced to look up. I yanked Escott back, maybe a little too hard despite my current state. He nearly lost his feet as I dragged him into the thin cover of some trees. He choked off his protest and followed my example of crouching behind the thickest trunks.

"What is it?" he hissed.

I pointed. One block over, waiting for a stoplight to change, was Emily Francher's white Studebaker. Inside it was Jonathan Barrett, looking impatient. The signal turned green and he plowed ahead in the direction we'd just come from.

Escott had seen the car, but his eyes hadn't picked up on the occupant. I filled him in.

"He's headed for the funeral parlor," he said.

"Probably to finish off what he started last night."

"I think we're safe enough for the moment."

"Yeah, and I'm going to keep it that way. Let's go back to the inn and get your clothes and my trunk." I moved, trying to go faster than before.

He caught up easily. "Are you suggesting we do a skip?" The American slang jarred with his accent.

"Just for tonight. You can come back in the morning and square things up then."

"Would it not be better to simply square things up with Barrett tonight? We do need to talk with him."

"Like the *Titanic* talked with the iceberg? No, thanks, I'm not up to it."

He had more to say, but I didn't feel like an argument and urged him to hurry. We made the rest of the walk in ten minutes, but it nearly did me in. My headache was almost as bad as before, and I was so dizzy that Escott had to hold me up. It was in vain, though; the Studebaker had returned and growled to a stop on the street in front. Barrett got out and trotted up the steps of the inn. We watched and waited, but he never came out.

"He'll be up in the room," I said. "He'll be there the rest of the night."

"And you are in no condition to confront him. We can leave the luggage for the time being and shelter elsewhere. I've no objections to roughing it for one night."

"Roughing it?"

He took charge and helped me away to a small park close to the inn. We sank onto a stone bench in a dense group of trees and stared at nothing much for a time. It was too cool for crickets, but other night creatures moved around us; busy with hunting, feeding, and mating—busy with survival.

Escott was thoughtful. "If he asks for me at the front desk and they find I am not in my room . . ."

"You can fix it tomorrow."

"I wasn't thinking of the bill. When they open the parlor in the morning and find themselves one short, they'll come looking for me for an explanation. I was planning on having at least a partial alibi for my evening by spending it in the lobby again. Barrett has effectively prevented that."

"Then we get you another. Show me one of those watering holes you went to the other day."

"Are you really up to another walk?"

"It comes in cycles. Just keep it slow and stay out of sight of our window if you can."

He could. My head was not so dizzy now, but I'd soon want a place to stop and completely rest.

"Hand me that packet of earth," I said. He retrieved it from the bag and I shoved it inside my shirt and buttoned up again. It may have been a delusion, but I seemed to feel better having it next to my skin. "What's clinking in there?" I referred to the bag.

"Milk bottles, a large syringe, glass cutter, tubing, gloves—"

"Syringe?"

"For drawing blood. I found it at a local feed store. Some of the farmers do their own veterinary work."

"I thought you were squeamish."

"I am, very."

"So how'd you do that? Draw off the blood, I mean."

"My actor's training came in very handy. For an hour I pretended I was a vet and it worked. Be assured that I was quite ill after I'd finished and had the time to think about it."

Glenbriar was very close to the sound with a neat little bay and a sampling of bars and similar vice shops for weekend sailors. Escott picked a tavern called The Harpoon and led the way inside.

It was half for tourists, half for locals, with fake nets and stuffed fish on the walls, along with some other nautical junk. Escott bought a double something at the bar and carried it to the distant booth I'd picked out.

"Nothing for me?" I joked.

"This is as much as I wish to imbibe tonight," he stated. "There's little sense in both of us having a bad head." He sipped at the stuff—it was probably gin—and made a quick sweep of the other patrons. They looked like regulars, eyeing us once and returning to their own conversations. The bartender leaned on one elbow to listen to a man grouse about his wife.

"Real live joint."

"Better than the one you just left," he pointed out. "Would you care to tell me what occurred to you last night?"

I told him about the wrong road, the heavy rain, and how I found the cab. Shutting my eyes, I put myself there again and tried to repeat all of Banks's last words. "That's when I was hit. I must have gotten there right after it happened. Barrett saw my showing up as a piece of luck for him and he used it."

"Why are you so certain it was Barrett?"

"He knew to use wood, it had to be him. He also knew you were nosing around town and maybe found out that we'd questioned Banks. . . .'' I read his face. "All right, why are you certain he's clear?''

"I'll grant that he is the likely suspect and he is tall—Banks would see him as tall at any rate—but the forensic evidence would indicate otherwise.''

"Indicate what?''

"You and Banks had your skulls cracked by several heavy blows; I saw both of you today while the doctor was having his first close look. I don't believe Barrett did it because the blows were not heavy enough.''

"They did the job.''

"On Banks, yes, but not on you.''

"I'm different from Banks.''

"Exactly, and Barrett of all people is aware of that difference and would have allowed for it. Had he actually been wielding the murder weapon, he would have completely pulped your head to make absolutely certain you'd never get up again.''

"I damn near didn't, anyway. If they'd done an autopsy . . . he might have been counting on them to finish the job.'' My shoulders bunched up and my stomach felt like caving in again. "Besides, he might have held himself back to keep it from looking too brutal.''

"A single murder in this quiet pocket of the world is considered quite brutal enough, let alone a double one. In for a penny, in for a pound, you know.''

"What's your point, Charles?''

"My point is that whoever tried to kill you was *unaware* of your special condition.''

That hauled me up short. "Come again?''

He blinked. "I'd forgotten, you don't know the official theory on this.''

"What's the official theory?''

"That Banks picked up a fare who made him stop, bashed in his head, then robbed him. You arrived on the scene while the killer was still there and were attacked in turn.''

"A good Samaritan who got walloped himself?"

"Something like that. I believe the killer heard you speaking to Banks, or trying to, feared you'd get a clue to their identity, and decided to do for you as well."

"And they didn't know what I am?"

"Apparently."

"Which means it could have been a real robbery."

"I consider that to be a very small possibility, and so would the police if they had all the facts of our own investigation. We know Banks drove a woman from the Francher estate to Port Jefferson. Within twenty-four hours of giving us this information he is murdered. I believe the woman wanted him silenced, sought him out, and killed him."

I felt very tired. "Which means Emily Francher—"

"Or Laura."

"But Laura was only fourteen or fifteen back then."

"Yes, with some growing to do," he said meaningfully, only I wasn't up to catching on to it. "Banks said *change* and *tall*. If you speculate a bit on filling in the blanks, he might have been trying to say, 'She's changed, gotten or grown tall. She lied.' "

I shook my head, not the smartest thing to do. "What's her motive?"

"As far as Banks is concerned, she killed him to shut him up. She didn't want him to identify the person he took to Port Jefferson."

"Barrett could have hypnotized either woman into killing for him."

"That's a possibility. Our lack of data is most frustrating. If you've no wish to confront Barrett, then we must use this time to speak with the two women to find out what happened five years ago."

"I'll tell you what happened: Maureen got in that cab, went to Port Jefferson, and then to parts unknown. We show up way too late, ask some questions, and then some creep just happens to kill Banks and nearly gets me. We're trying to make this thing more complicated than it really is.''

He drank his drink, listening until I'd run down and was out of nonsense. ''Do you wish to drop this and go home?''

''I don't know . . . yes. I think so.''

He pushed the glass aside, got out his pipe, and spent some time lighting it. He puffed and played with the match stubs with an absent finger. ''I see.''

But he didn't, and I started up another protest, which he cut off with a raised hand.

''I see that you're tired, upset, and frightened.''

I glared at him.

''You've had too much coming at you in too short a time. Just because your physical nature has drastically altered is no reason to think your emotional nature shares the same advantages.''

Advantages. Is that how he saw it? Confined to the night, avoiding mirrors, always having to plan out the next feeding, worrying that someone might get too curious about the big trunk in the corner . . . The whole business stunk and I was stuck with it, maybe forever.

''I'm just letting you know that I'm aware of how it must be for you right now. I'm also letting you know that if you do decide to go home, I won't be coming along just yet.''

''And try to take on Barrett yourself? Maybe get killed? Is this some kind of blackmail to keep me here?''

''Not at all. What you decide for yourself is all right with me, and no hard feelings. My own decision is to stay. I can't leave anyway at this point. It might be open to misinterpretation by the police.''

A smile tugged at my mouth. ''Like charging you with body snatching?''

''I certainly hope not, but it is a possibility. They'll have no real evidence against me, of course, but I'll have to remain until they say otherwise. They could make a lot of trouble for me, and I've no desire to lose my license.''

His investigator's license wasn't the only thing that kept him going, though. He had the same kind of curiosity that often got me into trouble. In the last week, a lot of it had been burned out of me and I was having trouble handling it in another person. Answering questions solved problems for him; for me it only seemed to make new ones. The emotional cost was distressingly high.

"You know if you stay you could get yourself killed. Barrett can do it without even trying."

He nodded a little, his gray eyes yellow in this light. Of all people, he knew exactly what he was up against, and it still didn't seem to bother him.

My breath exploded out in a sigh. "All right. I'll admit I'm scared. I don't like what we're doing and what might come out of it, but we both know that only a real bastard would run out now, and I'm no bastard."

He put down the pipe, maybe a little relieved after all.

"But," I added, "I've finally figured out that you are, when you want to be."

His eyes flicked up in surprise and went totally blank for a long second. I thought my joke had fallen flat until an abrupt bark of laughter burst from him. Heads turned our way from the bar and he stifled it quickly and returned to his pipe.

"So what's next?" I asked.

"Next I think you should—" He froze again, this time looking past me at the door.

I was careful not to turn around. "What is it?"

With a minimum of movement, he shoved the bag with the bottle, tubing, and other junk across the table into my hands. "They can't see you yet, so you can safely disappear for a bit. Nemesis is approaching and you might be recognized."

I managed to vanish a second before someone large stopped at our booth.

"Good evening, officer," said Escott in an even, untroubled tone.

"Would you come with us?" It wasn't a question.

"Why? Is there something wrong?"

"Just come along, sir."

"I would like to know why."

A silence. The rest of the bar, as far as I could tell from my muffled hearing, was quiet. "We got some questions to ask."

Escott made a knocking sound as he emptied his pipe. "Can you not ask them here? I don't understand."

A second man drifted up next to the first, both looming over Escott. They weren't taking any chances. "We'll fill you in at the station. Come on."

There was some movement and more puzzled protest from Escott. I hoped he wasn't overplaying his innocent-citizen act as they led him out.

I followed, clinging to one of the cops until we got into their car. He sat in the back with Escott. Eventually he shivered and complained about the cold, so I shifted over to the empty front passenger seat.

Escott made another attempt to get information from them and subsided with obvious disgust. The rest of our short trip was made in silence.

After stopping, I lingered in the car long enough to materialize for a quick look as they marched Escott inside. The station was tiny. The front windows disclosed a one-room office with a desk, phones, and files. Through a wide heavy door in the back wall were the cells. The ones I could see were empty.

We were in Glenbriar's municipal district. Conveniently across from the jail was the courthouse and next to that an ancient structure claiming to be the city hall. Down at the far end of the street, I abruptly recognized the Glenbriar Funeral Parlor.

All its lights were on, blazing away like New Year's.

Oops.

8

I QUIT THE car, found a way around to the back of the jail, and slipped inside, too nerved up for the moment to worry about my sore head.

The place was all linoleum and painted metal; nothing to get excited about. The open door at the end of the cells led to the outer office, and I crept up to it with my ears flapping, only nobody was talking. I got in the angle created between the door and the wall and peered through the crack made by the hinges.

Within the narrow strip, Escott's profile and part of a uniformed deputy leaning his butt on a big desk were visible. The other man was out of view, but a squeaking chair placed him a few feet in front of Escott. They were all motionless except for breathing, and sometimes one of them turned that automatic body pattern into an expression of impatience by an occasional sigh. They made no offer to get coffee, which I interpreted as a sign of Escott's ambiguous status with them. A guest gets coffee and a prisoner you talk around like he's not there; Escott was neither and that put my nerves up even more. I couldn't tell what Escott was feeling.

A phone rang and the guy at the desk answered. He said, "Yeah," and hung up. Five long, silent minutes later a car rolled up and another man walked in. The deputies stood up and made room for him.

"Thanks for coming down, Escott," he said.

"I had little choice in the matter, Chief Curtis," was the dry reply. "What is this all about?"

"We want to know what you did with your friend."

"I don't understand."

And it went on like that until the cop got around to revealing the embarrassing fact that my body had taken a powder. Escott hadn't been kidding on his moral outrage. He was a real treat to watch, but Curtis expected an act and wasn't buying any of it.

"Put the lid on for a minute, Escott, and just tell us everything you've done today since four o'clock."

Escott choked a little. "You really think *I* did it?"

"You were the one so dead set against an autopsy."

One of the deputies snickered at the inadvertent joke.

"Yes, out of respect for his religious beliefs—"

"Which I think is a lot of crap. You know as well as I do we throw that out the window in a homicide case. Don't you want to find who killed your friend?"

"Of course I do—"

"Then tell us where you stashed the body."

"I didn't 'stash' it anywhere because I never took it. I've done nothing."

"Then tell us what you *have* done."

He gave out with a loose schedule of a walk around the town, dinner at the inn, and another walk ending with a drink at The Harpoon. As stories went it was pretty lousy.

"Anyone see you on these walks?"

"I suppose so. I wasn't paying much attention."

"Did you go past the funeral parlor?"

"I did. It's on the main street and I recall going down that way once."

"Did you go into the parlor, like maybe to pay your respects?"

"No."

"Did you want to?"

"Are you charging me with anything?"

Curtis ignored the question and hit him with a dozen more of his own, which Escott handled the same way; the truth, but not all of it. If I hadn't been the missing body all the fuss was about, I'd be starting to believe him.

I wanted a look at Curtis and chanced taking a peek around the other end of the door. It was safe enough, one man was watching Escott and the other was out of sight.

Curtis was smaller and slighter than his help, but with the kind of tough stringy body that reminded me of tree roots. He had short gray hair, a narrow face, and wore steel-rimmed glasses that caught the light and hid his eyes. He looked like the kind of person who could spot a lie and be ready to deal with it before it was out of your mouth. Escott was in for a hard time.

The deputy glanced up and I ducked back behind the door. Talk lagged while he came across the room for a look. I vanished, sensing his close presence for a moment as he checked the cells and turned away.

"What is it, Sam?" asked Curtis.

"Thought I saw something."

He'd left the door wide open so it was flat against the inside wall and I no longer had a place to hide and watch. I shifted to one of the cells and materialized on the lower bunk. Escott's bag was still with me and I took care not to let the stuff inside clink.

Talk in the next room resumed. Escott stuck to his bad story, Curtis let him know in very precise terms just how bad the story was, and neither side gave an inch. Having been in the same situation only a few days ago, I was all sympathy. Too bad Escott couldn't hypnotize his way out of this one. I seriously speculated on walking in the front door with a sad tale of concussion and a family history of catalepsy and amnesia. The consequences would have been amusing, but maybe not too productive to a low profile. I was distracted from further planning when the station door opened and another man entered.

"Well, Doc?" said Curtis expectantly.

"Brought 'em."

A chair squeaked and bodies moved.

"Out with your mitts," someone instructed, and there was a concentrated silence. I whisked from the cell and peered past the door with one eye, trying to be thin. Escott was standing at the desk having his fingerprints taken. He was given a towel to wipe off the ink, but they ignored his request for soap and water. Curtis ordered him to be taken to the next room.

I jumped back into the cell, grabbed up the bag, and went away for the minute it took to lock him in.

"This is too bloody much!" he exploded as the key turned. "Am I under arrest? Answer me!"

I followed the deputy out as he shut the door, listening while they examined and compared. They were disappointed.

"Well, what did you think?" Curtis growled at them. "If he's smart enough to move a stiff and not be seen, he's smart enough to wear gloves. What about the others, Wally? Did McGuire take yours?"

"Yeah, and none of the prints match what we found on the table."

I grinned invisibly. Any prints on that metal table would be mine.

The doctor continued. "I'd just like to know why he did it, if he did do it."

"Who else? You said he threw a conniption when you started to cut."

"People are like that, they don't like to think about what we have to do. . . ."

"Like hell. This bird's no virgin, he's been in the business long enough. As for that religious scientist crap . . . he's hiding something."

"Then *you* try wearing him down. In the meantime I think

you should see if there're any students spending the weekend in the area.''

"Students?"

"As in medical. We got up to games in med school that would curl your hair.''

"Students?" Curtis repeated unhappily. He had badly wanted to pin it on Escott and now had a new distraction to trouble him.

"Where do you want this stuff?" asked Wally.

"In the file over there.''

Wally went over there and shuffled away the fingerprints.

"Now what?" asked the doctor.

"We let him wait and think. I'm going for my supper. I've been running my ass off since yesterday. Want to come?''

Curtis and the doctor left, and the two remaining men discussed their own dining plans. I drifted back to the cell, took the top bunk, and re-formed.

"You all right?" I whispered.

He was standing at the locked door, less than two feet away. He whirled, drawing a quick breath. "Not just then. You should knock or something, I nearly had a cardiac.''

"Sorry."

"Have you been here long?"

"With you all the way.''

"I thought as much when that deputy got cold and then started seeing things.''

"I just came from the other room. They were trying to match your prints with some from a table. I think it's the one I'd been lying on at the parlor.''

"With little success. I imagine the prints they found were your own.''

"That's what I figure.''

"I suppose I could suggest it to them. . . .''

"Don't be funny. The chief's gonna let you stew here for a while.''

"I expected no less. They'll have to release me in twenty-four hours, though, or charge me."

"Only if they're nice about it. Some of these small-town cops can be regular dictators."

"One can hardly blame them in this case, as they are very much out of their depth—"

The outer door opened and I got scarce fast.

"Awright," said the deputy, "who you talkin' to?"

"My lawyer, if I'm allowed the chance. Where is Chief Curtis? He can't just shut me in here without . . ." He went on and on until the deputy left, slamming the door on his tirade.

"All clear," he whispered.

I reappeared on the floor, next to the lower bunk with my back against the wall. He was still at the cell door, his fingers threaded through the bars. They weren't the vertical type, but inch-wide iron strips in a latticework pattern that made the dark cell a claustrophobe's nightmare. The walls and ceiling were metal as well and covered with institutional green paint marred by graffiti. It was thickest along the bunk wall, with the usual initials, scratches to mark off passing days, and a crude figure of a woman to remind inmates of what they were missing.

"Not too terribly cheerful, is it?" he asked, reading my face.

"I'll get you out of here."

"A jailbreak?" He shook his head.

"No, I'll find Curtis and have a little talk with him."

"I'd rather hoped you might. Are you feeling better?"

"Yeah," I said, with some surprise. "It's funny, but I think my disappearing act seems to help—like taking an aspirin."

He was interested. "You do look improved."

"Will you be okay here?"

"Safe as houses." He removed his coat, folded it neatly, and stretched out on the lower bunk with a sigh.

"But aren't you worried?"

"Over what?"

"If Curtis checks your story at the inn, Barrett could hear about it. You're a sitting duck in this cell."

"I'm aware of that possibility, but pacing and tearing my hair will not help the situation."

"You still don't think Barrett is behind any of this?"

"Before forming an answer, I need more data."

I let it slide for the moment. "Speaking of which, you haven't filled me in on what happened today."

"What about Chief Curtis?"

"He's having supper with the doctor. I can't do anything until there's a chance of getting him alone. I can catch him when he comes back."

He nodded, approving. "That will be Dr. Evans, who is also the local coroner. He fancies himself to be a criminologist—"

"And nearly sliced me up for salami from what I've just heard."

"Erm, yes. Well . . . the less said on that the better."

"Sure, but thanks for heading him off. So, how did you spend your day?"

He squeezed his eyes shut. "I have the strangest feeling of déjà vu."

"Maybe you could tell me how I spent *my* day instead."

He jumped at the chance. "To summarize: you and Banks were discovered at about seven forty-five last night by a Mr. and Mrs. Malloy. Malloy was reluctant to leave the scene, tried to flag down a passing car for help, and succeeded on his second attempt. He sent the driver on to call the police. They arrived and the official investigation began.

"The two of you were pronounced dead at the scene and photos were taken. The hurricane delayed things and it was several hours before they could move the bodies. The worst of the storm hit around dawn. I was awake at the time along with a few other guests and beginning to wonder what happened to you. I thought you might have found it necessary to go to ground because of the weather, or that the car had broken down someplace. A deputy showing up to drive me to the funeral parlor to identify your body was the last thing I expected."

"Did you think I was dead?"

"Not after I saw you, but I knew you weren't at all well."

"How so?"

"That horrible shrinking and aging had not set in, so it seemed likely you would recover, given time and a little help. I was then invited to aid the police in their inquiries—"

"How did they know to find to you?"

"They traced the registration of the car to its hire firm, then to our Manhattan hotel, and ultimately to the Glenbriar Inn. They were less than satisfied with my story of a vacation, but had to settle for it, as it was all the information I was pleased to give them. They released me and I returned to the parlor in time to begin the first arguments against your autopsy. Dr. Evans was exceptionally busy because of the aftermath of the storm, and that helped. All he managed to get into the record was that you were probably dispatched by a blunt wood instrument of some sort, and the odd fact that after a period of more than eighteen hours, rigor mortis and livor mortis had not set in. He was mightily puzzled over that."

"We'll just make sure we keep him that way."

"I'm all in favor of—"

The door crashed open and the deputy bulled in. I barely squeaked out in time.

"Where is he?" he yelled.

"What are you talking about?" Escott's voice was mild.

"There's a guy in here, I heard you gabbing. Where is he?"

Escott didn't bother replying to that one and the man tore the place apart, which didn't take long, since it was pretty short of hiding places. In the end, he took Escott from his cell and locked him into another.

"Anything, Wally?" he called to his partner, who was outside beating the bushes by the jail windows. Wally came back distantly with a negative answer.

"What is the problem, Deputy?" Escott asked, with the polite blandness one reserves for idiots.

"You shut up," he ordered, and marched out, leaving the office door hanging wide open.

I resumed shape in the most sheltered corner of Escott's new cell. His face was grotesquely crisscrossed by the shadows cast from the bars, but he was silently and heartily laughing.

"Guess I forgot to whisper," I murmured.

He recovered enough to say, "We both did. I never thought jail could be so amusing."

"I'll get going before we drive them nuts."

"Good luck," he wished, and I winked out, taking the fast way through the front. Both men were very quiet and still, probably listening for more conversation from the cells. Unless Escott decided to treat them to a Shakespearean soliloquy, they were out of luck.

It wasn't late, but the streets were empty and had that post-midnight feel to them. Hard blue light from lamps around the station picked out broad puddles left by last night's storm, and a cool wind made the water shiver and stirred fallen branches. Not feeling it even in my thin shirt, I stood motionless under the shadow of a tree. I had nothing to do but wait and hurt and think and grieve. Down the block the windows were still lit at the funeral parlor where John Henry Banks waited to be buried.

A slow hour passed before the chief's car chugged up to its slot in front of the station. He was alone, which was exactly what I wanted. As he got out, I put myself on the sidewalk and called to him.

"Chief Curtis?" I used a light, friendly voice. I was someone with no real problems or gripes.

The car was between us. He shut the door and looked up. "Yes? Who's there?"

That reminded me about my superior night vision. He was squinting to see my face against the harsh, inadequate light of the street lamps.

"I need to talk with you, if you have a minute."

He didn't know my voice and was trying to place my body shape, comparing it with others in his memory to identify me. I was familiar, but he didn't know why.

"I got a minute, come into the station." He remained on his side of the car, unconsciously on guard. Some deep instinct within had raised the tiniest of alarms. I rounded the front of the car—a natural enough move—but it put the light squarely behind me and kept my face in shadow. His glasses picked up the brightness and threw it back.

"No need to go to any trouble, sir, I just had a question for you." I was almost close enough to start, but had to move to one side so he could see my face, half in light, half in shadow. He didn't know me, but I was now very different from the rain-sodden corpse on the roadside under the glare of his flashlight.

"What is it?" He was expectant. In another second he'd be impatient.

"I want you to listen to me," I said, focusing onto him.

Light flared over his glasses as I closed in.

The stone bench was cold and unforgivingly hard, but Escott cheerfully maintained its superiority over his padded bunk at the jail. His vest and coat were tightly buttoned and he was pretending not to feel the chill in the wind as we sat watching the Glenbriar Inn. The white Studebaker was still where Barrett had left it hours earlier.

My head had started its dizzy thumping again, adding to my worries. I hugged my precious packet of earth and longed for total rest deep in my quiet trunk. Chief Curtis had been less trouble than I'd anticipated, but it had been very draining.

A minute after I'd finished with him and faded into the night, he shook himself and completed the journey from his car to the station, unaware of its interruption. Escott was brought from the lockups and released, much to the puzzled annoyance of the deputies. Sometime tomorrow Escott would return to collect his car keys and my personal effects. I could have managed it all tonight, but didn't want to push things too far or too fast. There was always the chance that Curtis could be talked out of my influence by some familiar, sensible voice.

"I'm going inside," said Escott. His tone was relaxed and conversational, as though he'd only commented on the weather.

From this end of the place we could see the window of our room. If Barrett was up there instead of in the lobby, he hadn't bothered with the lights. I could easily imagine him sitting very quietly in the dark, facing the door and waiting for it to open. Escott had made his mind up and nothing short of my hypnosis could change it. I wasn't going to do that, but I couldn't let him go up there alone, either.

"All right." I stood up. Slowly. The nagging dizziness made the ground lurch. I'd used up a lot of precious energy dealing with Curtis.

"You don't have to, you know."

"I know. Let's get moving."

We left the park, going the long way around to avoid being in direct sight of our window. I kept my eyes wide open as we approached the back door to the inn, scouting likely corners and shadows for his presence. The memory of that amorphous gray blob so invisible to human eyes was still with me.

He was in the room and heard us come up the stairs. He could distinguish us from other guests by the sound of two pairs of feet, but only one pair of working lungs. Our door opened suddenly and he stepped into the hall to look us over with his candle-flame eyes. He nodded and stood to one side, inviting us in.

Damn few things ever ruffled Escott; he murmured a polite good evening and did so, turning on a light. It took me a little longer to follow.

Our room was undisturbed. If for any reason he'd bothered to search it, he'd been careful. Without thinking, I went straight to my trunk and sat on it; the soil within tugged at me like a rope. Escott sank onto one corner of the bed nearest the door and Barrett took a hardwood chair next to the window.

"I read the paper," he began. "I read all about the double murder and saw the name John R. Fleming, so I thought I should check it out and see if it was you. I'm glad you're all right."

My face must have been stone. "Are you?"

His lips thinned and his own expression hardened. "Yes, I see that you are. I'll go now."

"Wait." Escott arrested his move to leave. "Something else must have brought you here as well."

"It was the story in the paper," he stated, his voice even.

"Indeed."

Barrett didn't like his look and started to rise again, and again Escott stopped him.

"The other man who was killed, John Henry Banks—what do you know about him?"

"Only what they said in the paper. Why should I know anything about him?"

"He was the man who chauffeured Maureen away from the Francher estate five years ago."

The revelation did no more than raise one eyebrow. "He was?"

"We spoke to him at length. He remembered a small woman wearing a veiled hat who hardly spoke to him."

"What a remarkable memory he must have had."

"Only because of the unusual nature of his fare."

"How so unusual?"

"Because it had been a very long drive for them and she bestowed a rather large tip for his trouble."

Barrett shrugged. "It's a long road back to the city."

"But he did not take her to New York, he drove her to Port Jefferson."

"Port—"

"Why would anyone want to go to Port Jefferson?"

"To use the ferry to—" He broke off, his brows coming together.

"Would Maureen have had any reason to go to Bridgeport?" Escott asked, putting a very slight emphasis on her name.

"I don't know." He wasn't sure, though, and we both picked up on it.

"We saw you earlier tonight," I said. "You were going to the funeral parlor, weren't you?"

He all but grabbed at the change of subject. "Yes, when I read about your—your trouble. I thought you might need help."

"Did anyone spot you?"

He looked slightly embarrassed. "I'm afraid they did."

That explained why Escott had been picked up so fast.

"I got away and thought it best to come back here to wait for you."

"So you could be neat about things and take care of Escott, too?"

As a shock tactic it didn't work very well. He was surprised, but not in the way I'd expected. He gaped as though I was mentally deficient and looked to Escott for an answer.

"Jack believes you tried to kill him last night," he explained quietly.

Any breath in him had seeped out and he struggled to replace it to speak, only he couldn't speak. His face was eloquent. Unless he was a better actor than Escott, he was an innocent man. Innocent of my attempted murder, at least.

"No," he finally whispered. "Why ever should I want to kill you?"

Escott didn't answer directly. "Banks was the intended victim, Jack only arrived at the wrong time and was attacked in order to shut him up. He might have seen or heard something that would have identified the killer."

"Why do you think it was me?" he asked, honestly puzzled. "Is it because of Maureen? Because we were once lovers?"

I hated him for being right. I hated the thought of Maureen in his arms, holding to him, responding to his touch—however long ago it had been. I hated that when she'd been in trouble she'd gone to him for help and not to me. I realized with shame that I could hate her for that as well.

Escott shifted uneasily and I looked away from them until

the emotions cooled off. Given a chance, they lose their terrible intensity, but until then I'm not safe to be around.

"The paper said it was a robbery." Barrett was speaking to Escott. "You obviously don't think so. Why?"

"There's too much coincidence involved for my peace of mind. The day after we spoke with him, the man was murdered. I believe the killer found out about our investigation into Maureen's disappearance. That person did not want anyone looking too closely into things and cut off a source of information. This, of course, presupposes that Maureen is dead."

The only sound was Escott's heartbeat and the soft tick of his watch. Barrett was utterly still. Eventually he looked at me, hoping I'd deny Escott's words. I'd lived with the possibility for so long on the edge of thought that I felt nothing. Barrett had never once considered it and was having to deal with the idea as one solid blow.

He shook his head slightly, barely moving. "You think she's dead?"

I looked past him out the window, not wanting to see a mirror of my own old fears on his face.

"Why do you think that? Where's your proof?"

Escott stepped in and answered for me. "Jack has no other proof than his knowledge of Maureen and her feelings for him."

"But she was terrified of Gaylen, of facing her."

"If Maureen were still alive, she'd have returned to him despite Gaylen's possible interference." He switched back to me. "She loved you, Jack, she would have returned to you."

I nodded my thanks to him for that piece of comfort.

"Then who killed her?" asked Barrett. "If she has been killed."

"You could have."

Barrett wasn't threatened by the accusation. "Why should I?"

"To maintain your position in the Francher household?" he suggested. "Maureen could have upset that for you, especially if she ever suspected you of setting the fire that killed Violet Francher.''

I felt the wave of pure shock roll from Barrett and flood the room.

"Easy, Charles . . ."

Escott was staring at the deceptively simple quilt pattern on the bed, using it as insulation between his mind and Barrett's feelings.

Barrett said clearly and slowly, "The fire was an accident."

"And a very convenient one for you, was it not?"

He was up and across the room faster than thought. All I could do was stand and take a step toward them, knowing that I'd be too late to prevent anything. At the most I might just be able to pry his fingers from Escott's broken neck, and I wasn't sure of doing even that much in my condition.

But Barrett stopped and did nothing more than stand over him. Unmoved, Escott continued to study the quilt, and Barrett's fists trembled for want of action.

"It probably was an accident," Escott continued, "and if not, then it was someone else who arranged it, not you. You have other means by which you may deal with such awkward problems. We know that. It would have been child's play for you to have influenced Violet Francher into accepting you. Why did you not do so?"

The answer was slow in coming, Barrett was still dealing with his emotions. "Emily asked me not to, and after my experience with Gaylen it seemed best to allow things to run their natural course."

"Did you know about the psychiatrists being brought in?"

"Yes, and if it came to it, I was more than ready to influence *them*. How did you come to know all of this?"

"Servants' hall gossip can be most enlightening."

Barrett snarled something obscene and returned to stand behind the chair, resting his hands on its tall back. I withdrew to the trunk. If he'd wanted to kill, he'd have done it by now.

"What was Emily's reaction to her mother's death?" asked Escott.

"What do you think?"

"I'm asking you."

"I don't know how to answer."

"Was it normal grief?"

"What's normal? I don't know."

"I think you do."

Barrett appealed to me. "How do you put up with him?"

"I usually tell him what he wants."

He shrugged. "For what it's worth, Emily took it very hard. She all but fell apart on us. Why do you ask?"

"Because she could have killed her mother."

He smiled. "No, that's impossible."

"You are very certain."

"I am absolutely certain, I was with her that whole night."

"But not during the day."

"No, but—"

"She could have rigged it all during the day, delaying things."

"No." He shook his head decisively. "No, she couldn't have done anything like that. You're completely wrong there. The fire started because of an old lamp wire shorting out."

Escott nodded, encouraging him to go on.

"Emily knows nothing about mechanical things. She's always had servants to do everything for her. She only has the vaguest idea of how to change a light bulb. Last year I tried to teach her how to drive and she was utterly hopeless at it. Besides, she's too gentle of heart. She could never kill anyone, nor even think of it."

Escott tilted his head to one side, looking directly at him. "Besides, it was an accident, as you said."

He scowled, knowing that Escott was patronizing him. "Why do you insist it wasn't?"

"Because it brings sense to what followed after: Maureen's disappearance and *why* she disappeared."

Things tumbled and lurched inside me that had nothing to do with my injured head. "Charles . . ."

He looked at me.

"No more," I said. "Leave it as is."

"You won't, by God," said Barrett. "You'll be telling me, and the sooner the better." His voice was low, but he meant every word and would tear it out of Escott if he thought it necessary.

"I can only tell you what I've been able to deduce from the inadequate data I have at hand."

"No, Charles. What's the point? What's the good of it? Maureen's dead, this won't bring her back."

"I know." He was surprised, but not offended at my attitude. "Maureen, Banks, and nearly you—who's next? *That* is the good of it. That's the purpose and point, the one that I have to justify it all for myself—to stop her from killing again."

"Stop who?" Barrett demanded.

Escott started to speak, but his words could mean his own death, so I interrupted. "He's not talking about Emily, but Laura."

Her name echoed silently on his lips. The color had gone out of his already pale face, leaving him a cold, bloodless statue until he began to shake his head again. "No. You're both wrong again. You're too inept to find Maureen, so you invent nonsense to excuse your lack."

"Was Laura home last night?"

He stared me up and down, then sense and disbelief took over, and he smiled. "You're wrong, laddie. What you're thinking is impossible."

"It is not," said Escott. "Very sadly, it is not."

Barrett's finger found a seam in the wood of the chair back where two different grain patterns met. He ran the edge of one nail along the join, unaware of the nervous movement. "Right, I've nearly had my fill of this. Come and finish your terrible tale."

"It *is* terrible," Escott agreed. "And I am sorry to bring this upon you."

"Get on with it."

"I will speculate that in 1931 a fourteen-year-old girl returned to her adopted home for her school holiday and found herself in the middle of a very tense emotional situation between yourself, Emily, and Violet. Laura did meet you for the first time that spring, Mr. Barrett?"

He nodded.

"Did she like you?"

"Yes, but you know how schoolgirls are."

"Schoolgirls grow up to be women. A person's age does not invalidate the depth or sincerity of their feelings—you can certainly understand that from your own experience. You may not have been interested in her then, but she was interested in you. Is that correct?"

"She may have had an infatuation, puppy love—"

"And Violet was trying to send you away." Escott held up his hand to stem any comment. "We'll pass over the subject of the fire. Whether or not it was an accident, it happened and removed any threat to your remaining on the estate. From Laura's point of view, there was the secondary advantage that she no longer had to return to school. She was needed at home to help care for her grieving cousin.

"It was probably the best summer she'd ever known . . . and then one night another woman came into the house—a former lover, and a woman you were still very attached to in ways that Laura could only understand by instinct. You invited Maureen to stay as long as she liked."

"You're saying Laura was jealous of Maureen, but not of Emily? The girl wasn't deaf or blind, she knew we were sharing a bed."

"Emily was also much older looking than you. To Laura's young eyes she was no competition at all, but Maureen was young, beautiful and well acquainted with you. Laura must have eavesdropped on some of your conversations together, enough to see her as another threat."

"And for that you think she killed Maureen? Is that the whole miserable story?"

"The most important part, yes. Was Laura then aware of your nature?"

"She knew only that I was allergic to sunlight. Some people are so and are not vampires—"

"But what might she have heard if she'd been listening to you and Maureen?"

Barrett shut up. His face pinched in thought, he paced the room up and back, then sat in the chair. "Go on."

"She apparently learned enough from the two of you to figure things out easily enough. If there is anything like a decent library in that house she'd be able to pick up some basic data about your condition and your special weaknesses. She would know how to take advantage of them."

"But she was a child."

"And very intelligent? Precocious, perhaps?" Escott's voice dropped to a gentle, toneless murmur. "Sometime during the day she murdered Maureen."

"She did *not*! Maureen left the next night. Mayfair saw—"

"Mayfair and Banks only saw a woman wearing a hat and a veil; a hat to cover her blond hair and a veil to conceal her face. A woman was seen arriving on the estate and a woman must be seen to leave. There was no reason for Maureen to want to go to Bridgeport. Can you think of one for Laura?"

"Her boarding school is in Connecticut," he whispered.

"The route would then have been a familiar one to her and a logical one for her to choose because of its familiarity."

"How would she get back?" I asked him.

"She must have hired another cab in Port Jefferson. We only failed to find it."

"And what happened to her trunk?"

"I don't know. We shall have to ask her."

Barrett had been staring at the floor and looked up after he noticed the silence. "What?"

"I said we shall have to ask her."

It took a while to sink in and he was shaking his head

slowly but decisively. "No. You're not going anywhere near her. You're both going to leave us all alone."

"And if we leave you alone, what will you do?"

But he wasn't ready to consider that. "No, you just get out of here and leave us."

"She's murdered two people, Barrett, possibly three."

"She has not. You've no proof for any of this. Only speculation, and what good is that?"

"Where was Laura last night?" I asked.

"At home in her room," he said too quickly, then realized it.

"What time? Was she in her room at seven-thirty or taking a swim? Was she out shopping or visiting a friend or just taking a drive in a hurricane? Or just maybe she was swinging a club at the back of Banks's head. There was a lot of blood . . . did she get it all off? Did the storm wash it away before she got home? Was her hair dry by the time you went up to her? Was she even in the mood for your company? Or maybe she was all excited and needed you to help work it off—"

The shock had come back to his face, then it swiftly evolved into white-hot fury. He was in front of me in one step, hauled me up, and knocked a fist square into my face before I could vanish. The room swung sharply to one side and a wall slammed me hard all over; or the floor, or both. I didn't care. Maureen was dead and I didn't care about anything at all.

9

"FINE," I SNAPPED, and wondered what the question had been.

"Yes," said Escott. "Now hold still."

He was kneeling over me, undoing my collar button. Only an instant ago he'd been sitting across the room. Not even Barrett could move that fast.

The ceiling, which seemed very far away because I was flat out on the floor, twisted every time I blinked. I shut my eyes hard against the effect.

"This is getting to be a very bad habit with you," he chided. "Are you the sort who goes in for self-punishment, or are you just naturally stupid?"

There was no reason to answer that one. "Where's Barrett?"

"Halfway home by now. You provoked him into a fine temper by that last display." He punched at my tender forehead with a dripping washcloth.

"Ow!"

"Serves you right. I was going to talk with him and get him to see reason, but you've effectively canceled that gambit."

"So buy me a hair shirt."

He dropped the cloth smack onto my face and got up in disgust. I rolled to my left side, using my arm for a pillow.

That damned hammer and anvil were at it again, and some thick, viscous liquid was sloshing messily around between my ears—probably what was left of my brain.

"What time is it?"

"After two."

Not late at all; five whole hours to sit around, stare at the walls, and wish I'd stayed in Chicago. Maybe I'd conk out regardless if I crawled into my trunk earlier than usual. Suppressing a moan, I eventually sat up, putting my back to the wall. It really wasn't as bad as my initial awakening in the morgue. I'd had worse hangovers when I'd been alive. Mentally I did want a drink, something 150 proof and painless till morning. I toyed with the idea of finding some animal, getting it stinking drunk, and then with all that booze in its bloodstream . . .

Someone rapped on our door.

Escott glanced at me. "Can you disappear for a moment?"

Why not? It was easy enough. No movement was required and therefore no real concentration; I was there one second and gone the next. The body with all its hurts was gone, gone, gone. Too bad I couldn't do the same for the mind and its memories. It was tempting to stay this way forever; floating, formless, and insulated from all the ills caused by living, simple living.

The rap came again, and Escott answered. His visitor sounded diffident but official. ". . . heard a crash and asked us to check on things."

The neighbors had complained to the manager about the noise. At two in the morning, you could hardly blame them.

". . . frightfully sorry, my own clumsy fault. I tripped rather badly."

"You're not hurt?"

"It's really nothing, bang on the shin. More din than damage."

"We just wanted to be certain . . ." And the man apologized for the intrusion and expressed sympathy for my tragic death, and had the police found out anything?

"They said to expect some new developments anytime now."

Which was a diplomatic way of describing my body being absent from the funeral parlor. Tomorrow's paper would make interesting reading unless Chief Curtis decided to keep it all quiet out of sheer embarrassment.

"Can we expect you to be staying with us much longer?" He was not overly enthused, even less so at the affirmative answer. It's bad for business when guests get themselves murdered. Escott bade him good night and locked the door. Reluctantly, I faded back into reality. The aches returned, but they weren't as sharp as before.

Escott dropped onto his bed and pinched the bridge of his nose. For the first time I noticed the blue circles under his eyes and the general slow-down of his movements. He'd been up most of the night because of the storm, and then spent the day fending off the police and waiting for me to wake up, either as myself or as a brain-damaged responsibility he didn't need. The last twenty-four hours had sucked the energy from him.

"Sorry about all this," I said lamely.

He considered my own forlorn form, shrugged, and accepted the apology. "We're both tired. Tell me, was that show pure temper, or had you a purpose in alienating the man?"

"It was temper, but I had some idea it was the only way to reach him, to get him to see her through our eyes."

"There are subtler ways of doing it," he pointed out.

"I'm not so good at that."

"Evidently."

"What now?"

"Some rest. I want to give Barrett a chance to cool down."

"What's to keep him from skipping town between now and tomorrow?"

"That is not too likely, as it would be an admission of guilt and leave Emily and Laura undefended. I believe the man has a streak of honor in him."

"Or he could skip with both women and we never hear of them again."

He shook his head. "I don't read that off him at all."

"That streak of honor?"

"Exactly. I believe that once he realizes the truth for himself, he will want to do the right thing. He only needs the time to think it all over."

"You figure he'll talk to Laura?"

He had a look in his eye that made me feel cold inside and out. "I am absolutely counting on it."

"I'll go out to the estate tomorrow and see what's happened."

"May I come along?"

"Yeah. I might need you to scrape me off the pavement again."

We'd planned to leave for the Franchers first thing, but he wasn't in the room when I woke up. It looked like the start of another disastrous evening.

I quickly dressed and stepped out to look for him, but being officially dead put a hell of a crimp into things. Walking up to the desk clerk to ask a simple question would only put the man into hysterics. While I dithered in the hall someone behind me said *psst*.

"This way," he whispered.

The top of Escott's head was just disappearing down the backstairs. He'd gotten the car back and had left it in the gravel lot with the motor running. We piled in and he ground the gears to get us moving again.

"Glove box," he said, before I could ask what was going on. His eyes were fever bright and there was a new tenseness to his body.

I opened the box and thankfully resumed ownership of my wallet, watch, and other junk. "This isn't the road to the Franchers'."

"I know, but something's happened." His lips had thinned to a single grim line and there was a brick wall behind his eyes.

"What?"

He tossed a folded paper in my lap. "The story's there. Emily Francher died today."

And he didn't say anything while I gaped first at him and then at the paper headline. The words swam. I couldn't make any sense of them. "What happened exactly?"

"I don't know, I've only just found out. There was some kind of an accident early this afternoon—a fall down some stairs."

"Shit. Where are we going?"

"The funeral parlor. For obvious reasons I daren't make myself too noticeable there, but you can get inside for a quick look."

"I'm not sure I want to. What am I looking for?"

"Any sign of Emily Francher's resuscitation or resurrection, or whatever you call it."

"Oh, Jesus."

"No need to be blasphemous, I only want your opinion on her condition."

Maybe he thought I was some kind of a vampire expert, which was true in a way, but I was not overconfident. "What if she has changed?"

"Then she might require assistance from someone who's been through it before. You said your own experience left you in quite a state of shock."

That was for damn sure. The night I had woken up dead, it took a hit-and-run murder attempt with a Ford to finally jolt my mind back into full working order. "What if Barrett shows up?"

"Tell him the truth of why you're there."

"And maybe ask if he's spoken to Laura yet?"

"I'll leave that to your discretion."

He dropped me in the street behind the parlor and promised to swing back again in fifteen minutes.

They'd replaced the window Escott had worked on with his glass cutter, but I had no trouble slithering through the cracks between the sash and the sill, emerging out of the air onto the sanitized floor of the morgue. I recognized the place with an uneasy twinge and was thankful it was empty. The adjoining office was also unoccupied, but not the whole building. Voices were coming from somewhere out front and I followed the sounds, tracing them through a bare linoleum hall.

Two wide doors opened onto a plusher room filled to the ceiling with the ultimate in vampiric clichés. They were stacked three high, and the ones on the bottom were tilted slightly with the lids up so that you could appreciate the linings. I counted nearly two dozen coffins, each with different styling, details, and prices.

I'd had no idea so much choice was available, from a simple native pine to a mirror-polished ebony with gold-plated handles. The one with scenes from the Sistine Chapel painted all over it with porcelain angels on the corners seemed overdone, but to each his own. I wanted none of it, preferring my cramped and homely trunk to such a constant and forceful reminder of death. The sight of a child-sized coffin and a tiny baby casket in a corner raised a sudden lump in my throat and I knew I had to get out of there.

The opposite set of doors led to a wide hall, this one with a white-and-gold carpet leading to the main chapel, or whatever it was. The walls were presently devoid of religious symbols, though I'd noticed a number of crosses, crucifixes, and even a Star of David leaning against a wall in the office. They were ready for all comers.

The voices originated from this room, where a man and woman were setting up folding chairs in neat rows. They were careful to stagger them so everyone would see the show up front. The line of chairs closest to the speaker's podium were fancier and non-folding. Painted white, with gold velvet upholstery, they were obviously reserved for the family. On a low, gold-draped platform left of the podium was a coffin.

The two people, apparently husband and wife and owners of the business, were busy discussing personal economics.

I'd expected them to be quiet or reverent or something as they worked, but life goes on, even for funeral directors.

Clatter.

"I don't see how another dime will really hurt us," said the wife. "It's only one more dime a week."

Clack-clatter.

The man shook his head. "That makes for five-twenty a year on top of what she already charges. You've got to look at the whole picture."

"Four-eighty at the most, dear. There are no lessons on the holidays."

"It's still four-eighty."

"But think of the savings later, when she can play during the services. Then we won't have to hire Mrs. Johnson to do the music. This is actually a kind of investment. Besides, the extra business we've just gotten *more* than covers the expense for . . ."

Clatter-squeak.

The last chair finally went up and they left by a different door, still talking. I slipped across the room.

Escott had jumped the gun on things. The body in the casket wasn't Emily Francher, but John Henry Banks.

Sometimes they look like they're asleep, but sleeping people usually have some kind of an expression. Banks looked the way he was—dead. They'd cleaned him up and there was no visible sign of injury, but he wasn't going to smile or exclaim over a generous tip ever again. The responsibility stabbed at me as it had at Escott, and I was torn between sorrow for Banks and anger at the person who'd killed him.

I paid what poor respects I could and left before the man and woman returned.

Escott rolled up and I got in. He found my report a disappointment, but got us moving in the right direction, toward the Francher estate.

"I expect that she left very clear and specific instructions concerning the disposal of her remains," he said.

"You can make book on it. I want to know exactly what happened and to see how Barrett is taking all this."

"Yes, and Laura as well."

I had some very private plans for Laura and saw no reason to tell him anything about them yet. "You don't figure Emily's death to be from natural causes?" He could tell that I didn't.

"I've no hard data yet to incline my opinion one way or another, whether it was an accident, act of God, or murder. However, it does look very odd, especially coming right after our interview with Barrett last night."

The town faded behind us and the trees drew right up to the road and closed overhead. Escott made the correct turning to take us to the Francher house.

"He might have questioned Laura," I said.

"Which is something else I need to know about."

"He may try to protect her."

"Protect her?"

"Not everyone is as justice minded as you, Charles. Like it or not, those two have become his family. A man will usually try to protect his family no matter what they've done. I'm just saying this as a warning. Barrett's got a hell of a temper and it could . . . could get away from him."

"As it has with you?"

I nodded, staring at the rush of gray shadows outside the window.

"Is that why you wanted to stop me last night?"

"Yeah, something like that. All I could see then was one big messy can of worms being dumped out."

"And what do you see now?"

"John Henry Banks lying in a box forty years too soon."

He drove quickly and absently, with most of his concentration directed inward and not at the road. He almost passed the gate by except for my warning.

Mayfair was just inside sitting on a camp stool, ready to handle the incoming traffic. He had orders that only officials of the law and family were allowed in, but Escott's investigator's license placed him nominally in the former category. That and a generous tip persuaded the Cerberus in baggy pants to let us through, and he even parted with some minimal information.

"She died from a fall down the stair in the front hall," Escott repeated, slamming his door and shifting gears. "One of the maids found her and thought it was a faint until she saw the blood. Dr. Evans was called out and he brought in Chief Curtis."

"Why the cops?"

"Mayfair didn't know."

"So maybe it wasn't an accident. Are they still here?"

"Left hours ago, but the relatives from Newport have arrived in force."

"How much inheritance do you figure is involved?"

He gave out with a short, cheerless laugh. "You and I think along similar lines. I've no idea, but it is bound to be quite a lot. I'd give a lot for a look at her will and how she may have allowed for things in the event of her return."

Cars were parked haphazardly along the drive and on the grass, and the garage exit was choked. Almost every light in the house was on, and faces appeared at the windows to inspect the latest arrivals.

A different maid let us in. She'd left off the white starched collar and cuffs of her uniform and wore unrelieved black. Her round mouth was crushed and her eyes were red lined and puffy from her own grief. I recognized her as one of the two women who shared rooms over the garage. She didn't bother to get our names, taking it for granted that Mayfair had kept out the undesirables.

Emily had a lot of relatives. Some of them might have been there out of genuine concern, but none were readily apparent. A lot of booze was flowing, so it was starting to resemble an impromptu wake.

"You see Barrett?" I asked him.

"No. Do you see Laura?"

"Nope. Let's split up."

"Right."

Escott melted away into the crowd and I lost sight of even his tall, distinctive form in a few seconds. The big front hall didn't look so big anymore; it was literally a case of all the world and his wife showing up. I started to push my way through a sudden opening when a thin, hard-faced woman with gingery hair focused her sharp eyes on me and came over.

"Are you family?" she demanded sweetly.

"No. Friend."

"Then you shouldn't be here," she quickly said. "It's family only until the funeral."

"How are you related?"

"Poor Emily was my cousin."

"Second or third and only by marriage," an eavesdropper put in helpfully, and got a drawn-daggers look for his trouble.

"We were *very* close years ago," she defended smoothly to me. "And *that* makes up for a lot."

"But never as much as you hope," added the heckler.

She turned her back on him to face me. "Anyway, you'll *have* to go. It's family only, as I said. The maid will show you out." She waited expectantly with her hands neatly folded and her chin up and I struggled not to laugh in her face. Someone else did, loudly, and was immediately shushed. This made us the brief center of attention and my reluctant hostess went very pink, but held her ground.

Someone else latched on to my arm and I thought for a second that I really was about to be evicted.

"Why, Cousin Jules! I haven't seen you since the war, how you've grown!" A younger woman in dark blue tugged hard and led me from the scene.

"Yeah . . . it's been a while," I loudly agreed.

Once out of immediate earshot she said, "Don't mind her, Abigail is just your average inheritance vulture like the rest of us. Her trouble is that she pretends so hard she isn't."

"Thanks, Mrs., Miss . . ."

"Clarice Francher, Miss." We shook hands. "I'm a vulture as well, but then I'm more honest about it."

"How's that?"

"I admit that I never liked Cousin Violet and hardly knew Emily. I'm here for appearance' sake and so I can hear what people are saying about me behind my back."

She was a pretty woman in her middle twenties with intelligent eyes and a nicely rounded-out figure. She gave me a once-over as well and seemed to like what she saw.

"And who are you, Mr. . . ."

"Jack F-flynn," I stumbled out, mindful that John R. Fleming was officially dead and had to stay that way for the time being. She picked up on the hesitation, so I changed the subject. "Look, I only just heard about this, can you tell me exactly what happened to Emily?"

Her big eyes had narrowed. "Are you a reporter?"

"No, only a friend."

"Whose?" She was evidently aware of Emily's hermitlike life.

"Emily's secretary."

This got me a second and much harder look. "Really? So the mystery man has a friend?"

I glimpsed Abigail from the corner of one eye, straining to catch every word. "Acquaintance might be more accurate." Someone caught Abigail's attention and she darted off to harp at them.

"Might it?"

"Yeah, we've got some business dealings in common. Now, about the accident—"

"Maybe you should talk to Mr. Barrett."

"I'd be glad to. Where is he?"

She shrugged. "Around, I suppose. I haven't seen him."

"I understand the police were called out here."

"Yes, they were, but it was just routine."

"Where did it happen?"

Clarice rolled her eyes, but with a hint of a smile. "You don't give up, do you?"

"It's what makes me so charming."

The smile became more pronounced. "All right. As I heard it, one of the maids found her at the foot of the stairs here in the entry hall. They called the doctor, but she was already dead—cracked her skull on all that marble. The doctor called in the police to look things over, but they didn't find anything funny. I think it was for show more than anything else. They probably wanted Laura to know they were on the job."

"Where is Laura? How is she?"

"Who knows? That tame dragon, Mrs. Mayfair, has been guarding her all day."

"When did it happen?"

"Sometime before two, because that's when the maid crossed the hall and found her. Good thing she did, or poor Emily might still be lying there."

"Where is she now?"

"They've put her in one of the side parlors." She nodded her head in the general direction.

"Would you mind taking me there, Miss Francher?"

"There're dozens of Miss Franchers here, you'd better call me Clarice." Somehow, despite her friendly smile, she made it sound like a threat. She linked her arm in mine again and we worked slowly through the hall. I got a look at the spot at the foot of the stairs and kept my eyes peeled for Barrett. The spot told me nothing, but the knot of people near it were entertaining and Clarice stopped to listen. Abigail was in the center of things, being her own sweet self.

"If you ask me, the little brat pushed her." She was obviously more candid and open with her opinions within the family.

"No one's asking you, Abby."

"Then you should. You don't know her, the stuck-up little bitch."

"Careful, Abby."

"What's the use? You know we're not getting anything from this because of her. If only cousin Violet were alive."

"We still wouldn't get anything, Emily's the one who got all of Cousin Roger's money."

"And she'll have left it to Laura or *that man*. He's nothing more than a gigolo, a fortune hunter."

"And what does that make you, dear Abigail?"

This brought about a furious response from Abigail. No one noticed as Clarice and I passed on to the parlor.

"They really shouldn't bait Abby so," she commented. "It's just too easy."

A corpse puts a damper on any party. As crowded as it was, no one was in the parlor when we entered. Clarice's fingers tightened very slightly on my arm as she reacted to the presence of death, and then let go.

Emily looked like Banks, dead. She wore some kind of white gown and held a white rose to her breast. They'd done a good job on her makeup; if she'd sustained any facial injuries or scrapes, they were well hidden. I looked long and hard, because her face did appear younger than I remembered, but she was lying down, and that would make a difference in the pull of the skin against the bones beneath.

The fine lines were still there under the powder, though. The mortician's artistry was simply undisturbed by movement or expression and gave only the illusion of youth. I touched her hand and said her name, but nothing happened.

She was cool, not cold; she'd been dead only a few hours. Her hand was still flexible. Rigor hadn't yet set in, but that wasn't unusual. It could occur anytime within ten hours of death starting in the jaw and neck, but I had absolutely no desire to test those areas.

"You liked her, didn't you?" asked Clarice.

I'd forgotten she'd been standing behind me and withdrew my hand from the casket. "I barely knew her, but I guess I did."

"A lot of us can say the same thing. Maybe if we hadn't been so blue nosed about that man she had . . ." She shrugged self-consciously.

"Yeah?"

"I don't know, maybe she wouldn't have been so alone in other ways."

"Did anyone in the family really dislike her?"

She was mildly surprised. "Not that I know of. There's jealousy, of course, but only because of the money. I think if she'd had a lot less of it, no one would have taken any notice of her at all."

"What about Laura?"

"What about her?"

"What's she like?"

She shook her head. "I saw her once as a kid at her parents' funeral. I really don't remember her. You sure you're not a reporter?"

Not anymore. "I'm sure. Thanks for taking me around."

"Leaving so soon?"

"I gotta look for a friend."

She smiled once more, her slight disbelief lending an interesting curl to the corner of her mouth. "Watch out for Abigail, cousin."

I craned a neck through the press outside for Escott or Barrett, and listened to bits of conversation as I made a way to the stairs again.

". . . call it a holiday? I tell you she had a complete breakdown and never got over it." ". . . wonder how much money she wasted on these trashy paintings?" ". . . the two of them carrying on with the girl right here in the same house." ". . . years younger than her, the poor thing, and it's not as though she didn't have a chance to find someone her own age." ". . . vicious old hag. Getting burned alive was only what she deserved. That's what they used to do with witches, you know."

A lowering of the general hubbub spread out from the center of the hall and heads swiveled toward a young woman descending the stairs. I didn't know her at first, but then the last time I'd seen her she'd been naked. Now she wore a severe black dress, and her lush blond hair was parted in the middle and drawn back into a demure bun at the base of her neck. She wore no makeup; her tanned face was drained and her eyes red.

"Laura, you poor dear!" exclaimed Abigail, and the thin

woman rushed up to be the first to take her hand. Laura looked at her blankly, forcing her would-be and now-embarrassed comforter to introduce herself. "But of course you must be exhausted," she concluded, to excuse the lapse of memory.

Mrs. Mayfair appeared and without seeming to, managed to disengage Abigail, and led the girl down to the main hall. As soon as there was space, whether by accident or design, several people closed ranks behind her, cutting Abigail off from further contact.

Laura didn't notice and was busy collecting comforting hugs and murmurs of sympathy from her more recognizable relatives. Once the "hello dears" and "we're sorrys" were out of the way, one of them voiced it for all.

"What are you going to do now, Laura?"

Laura shook her head and shrugged. "I have a lot to think about, but Mr. Handley is taking care of all the legal matters for now."

"We hate to bring this up so soon, but one has to be practical about such things. What arrangements did Emily make?"

"I-I don't understand," the girl faltered, looking very young and vulnerable.

"Cousin Robert is talking about Emily's will, dear."

"Oh. I hadn't thought about it. Mr. Handley—"

"Is a stranger. We're your family. You need someone you can trust. . . ."

They weren't making it easy on her. Mrs. Mayfair stepped into the breach. "Miss Laura is still very much shocked by the accident. She really should be upstairs resting."

Laura drew herself straight, remembering why she'd come down. "I-I just wanted to thank you all for coming. It is a great comfort, but I don't feel well tonight. Mr. Handley is here and he will answer your questions on . . . on things."

It had the sound of a memorized speech and generated some muted tones of disgruntlement. The girl was no fool and did indeed know where to place her trust. At this official statement, Handley came downstairs; a stocky man in a vested suit with a stubborn mouth and Teutonic jaw. He had the fixed smile of a hard professional and slicked his pale blond hair back with Vaseline.

"*Lawyers,*" hissed a woman, and made it sound like a curse.

"I know, darling," agreed another woman. "You can guess who's getting the lion's share out of this."

"Then there's no need for you to stay, is there?"

Handley said, "There are many arrangements to be made yet. Nothing can possibly be settled tonight, or at least until the poor lady has been laid to rest."

"He means we have to stick around till after the funeral to find out anything," a woman confided to her husband. She wrinkled her upper lip as though smelling a bad odor.

"When's that? Tonight?"

"*Shh*, Robert."

"This whole business is fishy—dead this afternoon and in her box by evening."

"Did you expect them to just leave her on the floor?"

"Miss Laura sincerely thanks all of you for coming and respectfully requests that you all return home until the funeral."

Objections rippled through the crowd. It was perfectly obvious to some that Laura's respectful request certainly did not apply to *them*. My sympathy went out to the hired help, who would have their hands full trying to evict them all.

Laura started upstairs for some peace, but Abigail had bided her time and darted in fast.

"My *dear* child, you really *shouldn't* be alone in this big house and you know that I—"

"Excuse me," I broke in, loud enough to distract even Abigail. "Miss Laura?"

"Yes?" Laura had a very kissable mouth and light blue eyes. Her pupils were dilated; Dr. Evans may have given her something to bolster her up for the mob.

"My name's Jack Flynn, I'm—"

"He's not family," Abigail put in suddenly. "He said so and

he told Clarice he was a friend of that—of poor Emily's secretary."

The information woke Laura out of her daze, or seemed to. Much of it might have been assumed as a protection against the emotional clawing and tugging from all the people around her. She studied me with guarded interest and not the least sign of recognition, but then whoever had slugged me on the road had done it from behind. "You're a friend of Mr. Barrett's?"

"A business acquaintance," I clarified. "I came to offer my condolences and see him, if I may."

"What business?" Her tone was dull, but now I was certain it was faked because of her question. She was interested and not content to fob this off onto her lawyer.

"Nothing to bother you about, you're quite busy enough." I was acutely conscious of all the curious eyes and cocked ears around us. "Is he around?"

Her answer was slow, as if she interrupted her inner flow of thought to remember my question. "No. Actually, I haven't seen him all day. Sometimes his duties require him to leave on short notice."

The hackles went up on my neck at her easy tone. "When did he leave?"

"I really don't know."

"Does he even know about the accident?"

She blinked a few times, as though confused. "Why, of course he does."

"Has anyone tried to find him?"

Her blank, frozen look was back. "Mr. Handley has. Perhaps you should talk to him. Would you please excuse me?"

Mrs. Mayfair got between us and took the girl upstairs.

Handley came forward, his smile still fixed in place, but not at all neutral. "What business do you have with Mr. Barrett?" he asked.

Again I was conscious of the audience all around us. "It's personal. Any idea where he is?"

"None at all, I'm afraid. It's very inconvenient for him to go off like this just when he's needed the most."

"And even Laura has no idea where he's gone?"

"None. He left no message, but Miss Laura has told me that it's not unusual for him to do so."

"I need to find him. Would the servants know?"

"You may ask them. Excuse me."

A dozen steps up, I caught him again. We were still very much in full view, but no one was in immediate earshot. "Don't you think it's odd, him being away like this?"

"A little."

"A little? The woman's private secretary takes off the same day she makes a permanent dive down the stairs, I think it's pretty damned odd."

"Are you suggesting some sort of connection?"

"Possibly. Did you know that they were lovers?"

He was quite properly shocked. "Mr. Flynn, I find your question to be extremely tasteless. To defame the character of my late client—"

"It can't be defamation if it's the truth. I want to talk to you about this."

His hard face got harder and the fixed smile twisted to express his distaste. "This way," he said in an acid tone, and continued up. I followed him to Barrett's office.

The rolltop desk was open now and littered with papers and ledger books. The French windows were also open to let in a faint breeze. Mindful of the veranda's connection to Laura's room farther down, I went out for a quick look. I was on edge not knowing where the hell Barrett had lost himself, and this was just routine paranoia—I really didn't expect to see the figure hiding in the deep shadows cast by the roof overhang.

10

HE WAS A perfect statue, standing exactly in line with a tall, potted plant. His subdued clothing blended with the darkness and made him as invisible to human eyes as anyone can get and still be solid.

The sight gave me a bad start and I had to choke back the surprise; then I wanted to belt him one for the scare. Escott read it all off my face easily enough and shrugged as though to say it wasn't *his* fault that I was so jumpy. He was there to hide from the lawyer, not to frighten poor nerved-up vampires.

"What is it?" demanded Handley, annoyed at the delay.

"Nothing, just checking the weather. We've been having an awful lot of it lately." I left the veranda to Escott and went inside to take a seat on the sofa. In order to face me, Handley had to turn his back on the open windows. He commandeered the banker's chair as I'd hoped he would.

"Now, what is this about?" From his attitude he must have thought I was warming up to try a little blackmail against the memory of his late client.

"Barrett and Emily Francher," I said.

"So I've assumed, since you suggested they had an intimate relationship."

"I stated they were lovers."

"Gossip is common, Mr. Flynn, very common."

"I know it for a fact."

"And have you evidence?"

"We're not in court, Mr. Handley, so just for laughs, let's pretend it's true. Can you think of any kind of errand that would keep Barrett away from here at this time?"

"He simply might not have heard the news yet."

"Laura just said that he had."

"Granted, but I can hardly supply you with the specific reason you seem to be looking for. Anything to do with the relationship of two people is bound to be complex, especially when such a disparate age difference is involved."

"More than you think," I muttered.

"What?"

"Nothing. Even with this talk of complexities, you think he'd run out at a time like this?"

"I really couldn't say."

"I'll put emotions aside, then. Let's say that his only attachment was to her money. There's a lot of it floating around here. I assume Miss Emily left a will?"

"You may assume correctly."

"Don't you think Barrett would want to stick around to hear it?"

"You presume that he is gone for good, young man. We don't know if he has. You also imply that Mr. Barrett is some type of fortune hunter, but I can tell you that Miss Emily was no fool in that regard."

"What do you mean?"

"Exactly what I said. Miss Emily was well aware of the kind of men who might prefer her money over herself, and allowed for it."

"I want to know what you mean."

"That is my business and none of yours, sir. Why are you so concerned?"

"Because I think it's damned funny that she should get herself killed at this time."

"What is so particularly special about this time?"

Watch it, I told myself.

"Are you suggesting there was something irregular about her death?"

"Convince me it wasn't. Convince me that someone didn't push her down the stairs."

He knew I was being utterly ridiculous. "Do you fully realize the serious nature of such a suggestion?"

"No one better. For instance, why did the doctor call in the police?"

"Miss Emily was a person of substantial standing in this community—"

"Bosh, she hardly left the house."

"She was certainly an important taxpayer, then. Dr. Evans called in Chief Curtis because he is a very careful, conscientious man. The nature of the accident was such that he wanted an informed professional to look at the scene in order to specifically allay the very rumors which you seem bound to spread."

"So he smelled something fishy, too?"

"That is not what I—"

"What'd the doctor have to say? And Chief Curtis?"

"You may ask them yourself, but I warn you now that if you are looking for some sort of cheap sensationalism in this tragic occurrence you are certain to be disappointed."

"Are you protecting Laura?"

"What do you mean by that?"

I was getting nowhere fast and lost my patience along with my scruples. "Handley, listen to me. Listen very carefully."

It was harder with some than others. He was on guard and didn't want to hear what I had to say, so I stepped up the pressure.

"This is very important. You must listen to everything I say. . . ."

He blinked once, twice.

"Listen to my voice. . . ."

His eyes softened, the stubborn expression gradually went

slack, and his world closed and centered on my words and
will. I told him to shut his eyes because I hate that dull look,
like what the animals get when I'm feeding.

Escott was peering around the edge of one window. I motioned him in, cautioning him to silence. He nodded and
came close enough to watch.

I kept my voice even and conversational. "Handley, do
you know where Barrett is?"

"No."

"What did Emily leave him in her will?"

"Nothing."

That surprised us. Escott impatiently gestured for me to
continue.

"Nothing at all?"

"No."

"What about for Laura?"

"Yes."

Playing twenty questions would take us all night at this
rate. "Have you a copy of Emily's will with you?"

"Yes."

That was a relief. "Where is it?"

"My briefcase."

Escott spotted the black leather case and made short work
of finding, drawing out, and unfolding the document in question. I left him to read it and kept Handley busy.

"What did the doctor say about Emily? How did she die?"

"She fractured her skull in a fall."

"Why'd he call the cops?"

"The man likes to dramatize, thinks he sees more than
what's really there." Handley didn't like Dr. Evans, either. I
wondered if he liked anyone at all.

"Did they find anything odd or suspicious?"

"No."

"What time did it happen?"

"About two o'clock today."

"Where was Laura Francher at two o'clock?"

"Outside. Horseback riding."

"For how long?"

"I don't know."

"Anyone witness this?"

"Haskell, the groom."

"Where were the other servants?"

The maid and cook were in the kitchen, repairing linens and baking bread respectively. Mrs. Mayfair was there as well, working with the cook on the week's new menu. The gardener was on the other side of the estate picking up storm debris. At 2:10 the maid finished her sewing and left the kitchen to take the linens upstairs. Instead of using the servants' passage, she went through the front hall to see if Mayfair had restocked the wood for the parlor fireplace. She found Emily at the foot of the stairs and raised the alarm. At some point in the proceedings, Mrs. Mayfair sent someone after Barrett. His door was locked and no one could find the key. They assumed he was out.

"You get all that?" I whispered to Escott.

"The germane points. Did Miss Emily not have a key to Barrett's room?"

I asked, but Handley didn't know.

"Odd, that."

"Not if Barrett wants to keep his secret. He'd have allowed for an emergency like this."

"Hmm. No doubt we can ask him. I should like to arrange an interview with this Haskell for the exact time of Laura's ride and where she went."

"If we can interview Laura, we won't have to."

"True." He skimmed the closely typed pages of the will. "I believe I see Barrett's guiding hand in this."

"Yeah?"

"There are some personal bequests, a generous trust for Laura, pensions for retired servants, and one most unusual arrangement. There is a long statement here by Emily concerning a close friendship she formed with one of her British in-laws. She had a special place in her heart for a young cousin whose name was also Emily.''

''You mean—''

He kept talking. ''In the event of Emily Francher's death, her secretary has instructions to contact this person. If she appears within one year after the reading of the will, the rest of the estate goes to her. This person's fingerprints are on file with the Franchers' bank manager and with Handley so that she may be correctly identified.''

''I can see the riot that's going to cause among her cutout relatives.''

''Yes, this is hardly something they'd lightly accept.''

''What happens if this other Emily doesn't show up?''

His eyes zipped back and forth. ''Then the estate goes to Laura. In the event of Laura's death, and/or if the other Emily never appears, then it's to be sold off and the money distributed to a number of charities.''

''You think Laura knows about this will? If she does, then she could have made an investment for her future.''

''Unless Emily's death was an accident, after all.''

''We'll find out.''

He looked at Handley with some amusement. ''I take it from your question to our silent friend here that you haven't found Barrett?''

''You take right. Nobody's found him. I'm thinking maybe he packed up last night and left.''

''Why should he do that?''

''I dunno, maybe he talked with Laura, heard something he didn't like, and took off to think things over.''

He folded the will and put it back in the briefcase. ''Did you see Laura?''

''Yeah, I even had a fast word with her. She gave out with a song and dance that he was gone because of his duties, whatever the hell that means.''

''She could be covering for him,'' he suggested.

''During the day, yes, but he'd be up by now. He might

just be wanting to avoid the relatives, and I can't blame him for that, but it looks bad.''

"True. I was considering that if Emily's fall were no accident, then Mr. Barrett is the only one in the house with no alibi.''

"Except with us. *We* know he couldn't have done anything.''

"Possibly. Can you guide us to his sanctum?''

"No sweat, but he won't want to see us.''

We started for the door, but Escott abruptly stopped. I didn't understand why until he jerked a thumb over his shoulder at the lawyer, who was still on the far side of dreamland.

"Handley? You can go back to your work, now. Completely forget we had this little talk, okay?''

"Very well,'' he replied, sounding perfectly normal. He opened his eyes, swiveled his chair around to face the desk, and started shuffling papers. Escott and I slipped out and paced down the hall.

"What were you doing in there?'' I asked.

"Virtually nothing, as I had no time to do it. I'd just gotten to Barrett's office and was about to search the briefcase when the two of you walked in. The rest of the time I was looking for Barrett. Were you able to get a look at Emily's body?''

"Yeah.''

"And her condition?''

"She's really dead, as far as I can tell.''

"Then God forgive me for not coming out here sooner.''

"You think it was no accident, then?''

"To do so would be to make an assumption without the benefit of facts.'' he said stiffly.

Okay, he had to be logical about things, but at least one part of his mind had given in to conclusion jumping, and he didn't like that part one bit.

We went down by way of the main stairs. People still loitered in the big hall, catching up on family gossip and speculating on their financial future. I was tempted to tell them all to forget it and go home.

No one paid any attention to us, and after a little thought I found the right hall and the right door, the only one in the wing that was locked. I slipped through it, found the stairwell we wanted, and came back again.

"No key on that side," I said. "I'll just—"

"I think I can manage." He pulled out an impressive set of skeleton keys and picks from a worn leather case. Crouching in front of the lock, he began to experiment.

"Aren't you the regular Raffles," I commented.

"Ah, but I hardly ever steal anything."

"Look, I can just go down for a quick gander. If he's really gone you won't need to—"

"There!" He turned the knob and pushed open the door. "That was a bit of luck. Usually it takes much longer."

"Where'd you learn to do that?" I was impressed.

"You acquire all kinds of skills in the theater." He replaced his picks and shut the case. "We once had a leading lady prone to the sulks and locking herself in her dressing room. For the duration of her contract I was often required to get her door open so the stage manager could persuade her to go to work."

"Crazy world."

"Very."

"But where'd you get that?" I gestured at the case as we went down the carpeted stairs.

"Oh, they're sort of an inheritance," he dismissed. "Let's see about this one now."

I didn't bother trying to slip through again; I enjoy watching an artist at work. The wood-covered metal door at the bottom of the steps had a different lock than the one in the upper hall and took longer to break, but it was fascinating to see him do it. He had a definite air of satisfaction as it gave way to his efforts.

Barrett wasn't there to greet us.

"Bolts on the inside I see," he noted as he walked in. "I suppose if he were still here he'd have shot them and your special assistance would be necessary, after all. This looks most ominous."

A few bureau drawers sagged open, their contents gutted, and there were gaps in the closet.

My shoulders were tightening and I didn't think it had to do with Barrett skipping out. Something else had crept into the back of my mind and I couldn't identify it.

Escott went to the library/living area and returned. "He's quite the reader. These books are well used. He also did a bit of writing . . . I've found some sort of journal. It's odd that he left so personal an item behind, unless he's on a short trip. . . . Where are you?"

"Closet," I called. The something bothering me wasn't in here.

He looked in. "Good heavens, it's as big as my sitting room."

I pointed. "He left his trunk."

"Perhaps he has a lighter one ready for travel purposes, as you do. That thing doesn't look too portable."

"Yeah, maybe."

"But I concede that this is also odd. You said he has earth in his bed?"

"Sewn up tight in some oilcloth." A scent in the air—that was what was nagging me. Each time I breathed in to talk . . .

Escott went over to the bed and flipped up the linens. Everything was in place as I'd found it a few nights ago.

"As far as we know, this island *is* his home ground."

I breathed, trying to catch it again.

"He might yet retain title to some house or—"

Bloodsmell.

"—plot of land in the area and could have gone there."

I drifted over to the bath, opened the door, and looked in.

"But the journal in there bothers me. . . ."

It was wrong. The whole damned world was wrong.

"Why should he risk leaving such a revealing document behind?"

And I was just another poor bastard with the bad luck to keep bumping face-on into the wrongness of it all.

"Jack?"

"Poor bastard . . ."

"What is it?"

Then he was next to me, staring at the awful thing on the cold tile floor.

"Oh, my dear God . . ."

The color left Escott's face and he put out a hand to steady himself against the wall. A return wave of last night's dizziness hit me and I backed from the doorway, staggering to the bed. The alien soil was no comfort.

Escott kept staring at it and I didn't like the look in his eyes.

"I should have anticipated this." His voice was very soft, very weary. "I should have. I've blown this whole business."

"Charles—"

He shook his head, quickly, to cut me off. He drew a steadying breath and went into the bath. After a moment he called out, "Jack, I want your help."

Jesus, for what?

Barrett had been pulled in feet first so that his head was just inside the door. He wore plain blue pajamas, but the top had been partially unbuttoned. The expensive silk was soaked through with massive patches of blood, most of it concentrated on his chest. Some blood was drying on the floor, but wide smear marks and two or three wet towels wadded in the tub indicated a little preliminary cleaning had been done.

Escott knelt over the body, his long fingers delicately peeling back the stiffening shirt front. The skin around the inch-thick shaft of wood in Barrett's chest was parchment thin and just as dry. He was like that all over. His handsome features had shriveled up like an old monkey's; his teeth were locked into a false grin by the lips and gums shrinking back. I was very, very glad his eyes were clenched shut.

"What do you want?" I asked.

"To render first aid."

"Charles, he's dead. He's probably been dead all day."

He shot me a piercing look, as angry as I'd ever seen him. "Knowing what you know, how can you tell?"

That shut me up.

He gave me a second to think, then said, "I need to try, I have to. Will you please help me?"

I gulped back whatever I'd started to say. God knows I owed him plenty, and he never asked for anything in return. "All right, name it."

Some of the tension left him. "I daren't pull the stake out until we have some blood on hand. He's very fragile now; the extra shock could be too much. My kit with the things I used to help you is in the car, along with that livestock syringe. Fetch it out and go to the stables—"

"But I don't know how to use a—"

"It's only a syringe. All you have to do is find a vein and push the needle into it. Pull the plunger back slowly, though."

I nodded doubtfully.

"The stable lad might be there. Svengali him if you must to get his help, but hurry."

I shoved down the sick hopelessness inside and got moving.

The front door was more direct and faster, but I didn't want to be seen, stopped, or questioned, and opted to disappear. I tore through the big hall, weaving between knots of dawdlers until I hit against the entry door and slipped through. Our car was way off to the left and I maintained that general direction awhile before going solid. The cloudy darkness made the possibility remote, but I was wary of being spotted from the house.

The car was standing alone now on the grass. It looked like a long night ahead and I didn't want anyone noticing it.

Escott had given me the keys, so I started it up and scooted over the grounds until it was hidden from the casual eye by a break of trees.

Escott had stashed the bag in the back. It contained everything but the syringe, which I found in a metal box that had slid under the seats. The thing looked huge, but then large animals can require large amounts of medication. I dumped the case into the bag and ghosted up the road.

Rounding the bulk of the house, I went solid and saw lights on over the stables. Haskell, the groom, was in. I trotted up the stairs to his room and tapped on the door, calling his name.

He presented a startled face, all suntan and mussed hair and wore only his undershirt and workpants. "Yeah, who are you? What is it?"

"I'm a friend of Barrett's. Listen to me, it's very important that you do exactly what I tell you. . . ."

He might have cooperated without my influence, but I couldn't waste the time answering his inevitable questions. By now I was long past the point of worrying about the morals of using forced hypnosis; it was a tool and it worked. I gave him just enough time to pull on his boots and sent him down to the fenced yard to bring in the horses.

My hands shook as I pulled out the syringe. It was one thing to use my teeth, and I had enough trouble handling that idea at times, but it was quite another to use a needle to do the same job. Escott wasn't the only one who could get squeamish.

Haskell led in a big roan gelding and tied its halter rope to a ring on the wall. Its ears twitched, but I soothed it down with a little stroking and talking. Horses like to listen to nonsense, and this one was in the mood for it. When Haskell led in a second horse I stopped him and held up a milk bottle.

"Can you find me more like this? Clean ones?"

He stared hard at it.

"Any kind of bottles?"

He finally nodded and I sent him off.

I crouched next to the roan, picked out a vein, and decided on a firm fast jab over a slow punch and managed to get it settled somewhere in the middle. I was clumsy and the horse felt it, but kept still while I filled the barrel of the syringe.

It seemed to take hours, but there was no way to hurry things. When it was full I drew out the needle, shoved the point inside the milk bottle, and pressed the plunger. The process was far too slow with the blood coming out in such a tiny stream; it'd take all night to get six quarts. From the look of Barrett's dried-out and shrunken body, he'd need every ounce and fast.

At the base of the syringe, where the needle attached, was a gizmo that unscrewed it, probably for cleaning. Trust Escott to think about neatness. I opened it up and poured the rest into the milk bottle, filling it halfway.

Just as I finished, Haskell returned, carrying a case of amber beer bottles.

"Those clean?"

He nodded.

"You make your own?"

"Me 'n Mayfair, but don' tell his missus."

"My solemn promise. Bring in the other horse, will you?"

He did and I worked. I was getting better at putting the needle in right, but no one would give me points for neatness or speed. But at least the milk bottle was full, now. It would give Escott something to start with.

"Haskell."

He let go tying a rope.

"You see what I'm doing?"

"Yes."

"Think you can take over for me?"

"Yes."

"Great. Just fill it up and unscrew this part to empty it into one of your bottles. Okay?"

"Uh-huh."

"And wash the needle clean each time. I'll be back shortly for more."

He took the syringe and I grabbed up the milk bottle and Escott's bag.

The door to the kitchen was open and lights were still on everywhere. Not knowing how I could freely trot through the house with such a gory burden and unsure about finding the right hall again, I went down the cellar steps for a shortcut. With the bottle and gear hugged close to my body, I walked through the thick brick wall into Barrett's room.

Escott was at the writing desk flipping through a book whose pages were covered with fine, script-style writing. His back was to me and yet again I gave him a start.

"What are you doing?" I handed over the bag.

"Waiting for you and poking into things." He put away the book and returned to the bathroom.

Barrett looked worse than I remembered. "How are you going to do it?"

"Tube down his throat," he said tersely.

"Was I like this when you found me at the warehouse?"

"Not as bad. I'll hold him still, you pull out the stake. Keep it as straight as you can."

I pulled. The brittle body vibrated. The wood shaft sang against the ribs and came free. Unbelievably, there was more blood left in him to well up in the wound. We both looked to his mummified face for any sign of life. He never moved. Escott grimaced and placed the tube between Barrett's teeth and fed it down his throat.

"Isn't it supposed to go up his nose?"

"The tissues are too shriveled to attempt it. The problem we have here is that his glottis might be open and I could end up putting the blood into his lungs instead of his stomach."

"You can't tell?"

"Not unless he's breathing." He fitted the other end of the rubber tube into a stopper with a hole in the middle.

"How'd you get by for me, then?"

"I was lucky."

"You learn all this at that hospital?"

"I picked up some useful knowledge during my brief sojourn." He shoved the stopper firmly into the bottle and up-ended the thing, pinching the tube slightly to regulate the flow. "Can you get more?" he asked.

"Yeah, Haskell's working on it. I'll be right back."

Haskell had the first of the beer bottles full and was busy drawing off more from another horse.

"You're doing a good job," I said. "Ever have to before?"

"Yeah, I know a little about this stuff." His tone was different. He'd come out of the hypnosis sooner than I'd expected.

"Are you all right?" I asked.

"Yeah."

"Do you know why you're doing this?"

"No, but I figure you're trying to help Mr. Barrett."

"You know about him?"

He glanced up and I could see there was a brain working inside his head. "Maybe as much as you do?"

"What do you know?"

He drew out the needle, detached it from the syringe, and carefully poured the contents into a bottle. "I know I got a steady job here, the pay is good, and I have a lot of free time. How many people can say that these days?"

"Then you've seen Barrett—"

He nodded, tapping in a final drop. "Yeah, he's careful, but I seen him a couple times down in the yard."

"Doesn't it bother you?"

He shrugged. "It scared me at first, but not now. He don't hurt no one, he don't hurt the horses. This is a good place to work and he's a nice man, you know?"

"What about Miss Laura? What d'you think of her?"

Another shrug. "She's all right, maybe a little too full of herself."

"How do you mean?"

"She's just not the type to think about others, but I guess she's still young yet."

I took the bottles to Escott. "Any change?"

"Look at his teeth."

I did. Barrett's piercing canines had been even with his others, but now they were more prominent, as though ready to feed.

"Of course, it might only be a reflex of some kind," he cautioned. "I don't want to get too hopeful."

"What about his chest?"

Escott's own heart was beating very fast. "The hole has closed up."

I felt a grin start up on my face. "I'll go get another couple bottles."

When I came back, there was a definite change in Barrett's appearance. His face looked fractionally fuller and the skin was flexible to the touch. "It's working, Charles."

He nodded, but his own expression was still tight. "You were a long time."

"I was having a talk with Haskell."

"Yes?"

"He said he saddled a horse for Laura at one-thirty, and then she asked him to wash her car. He'd washed it earlier that morning, but she gave him some guff about dust and told him to wash it again anyway. It kept him busy on the opposite side of the house and he didn't see where she went."

"Interesting."

"Yeah, especially when you realize she'd have no problem getting back into the house from a patio door on the far side. I checked—"

Barrett's body spasmed and he suddenly gagged on the tube down his throat. Escott quickly pulled it out.

"Charles, you're a goddamned miracle worker!"

His face flushed. "Some days are better than others."

Barrett's lips moved, his teeth still prominent. Escott put

the tube to them, but Barrett drew the blood out too fast and the tube collapsed from the suction. Escott detached it from the plug and put it straight into the bottle like a straw.

"We need more," he said.

"I'm moving."

In the end, Barrett drained away just over six quarts of the stuff, and I witnessed a faster version of the kind of recovery I'd gone through myself. The wrinkling smoothed, dry flesh-colored twigs turned into fingers, and stiff parchment filled out to became skin again.

He began coughing at one point, getting rid of the fluid that had built up in his pierced lung. It was a mess, but Escott grabbed a towel and I helped turn him on his side. The back of his pajama shirt was practically glued to the floor.

"How long do you think he's been here?" I asked.

"An expert could estimate from the condition of the blood, but I'm no expert. Perhaps it was concurrent with the incident on the stairs."

Barrett would be listening. Escott knew there was no need to hit him with the news of Emily's death just yet.

"Logically and practically, I would say it was done earlier, as this was a crime that was never meant to be discovered. Later than two o'clock and she would never have had the chance to be alone long enough to do it."

"And he's been here like this all day."

"He may not have been conscious."

He was only trying to ease my mind, but I knew better. Once his body had been dragged from the bed, Barrett's contact with his soil would be severed. He'd have been aware. Unable to act, but aware. For myself, there is no feeling worse than that kind of helplessness.

I stood and motioned Escott to come with me to the far end of the library, and kept my voice very low. "I need to go back upstairs again. Can you handle all this with him?"

"Yes, but—"

"I'm going to have a talk with Laura. It's way overdue."

"Agreed, but I'd like to be there myself."

"I know, but I need you to keep Barrett busy."

Whether he could read anything else into that, I wasn't ready to guess. The important thing was to say something that was halfway convincing so I could get out of there. He was distracted because Barrett was coughing and still needed help, otherwise I might have gotten more argument from him. Escott finally nodded, and if he knew what I had in mind, he chose not to comment.

"This might take awhile," I added, risking it anyway. A part of me hoped he would catch on and try talking me out of it.

He didn't, or wouldn't. "Very well. Take as long as you need."

I shut the metal fire door behind me and climbed the stairs up to the deserted wing. Inside me, equal portions of fire and ice went to war.

11

THE LAST OF the relatives were gone and the staff had cleared away their debris and swept up. Except for the stale stink of cigarette smoke hanging in the air, no signs were left of the recent invasion. I made a careful and quiet sweep of the place to make sure Cousin Abigail hadn't lingered in some corner, but all was clear and silent. In a den off the main hall I found a third of a bottle of whiskey in a liquor cabinet and took it upstairs.

The door to Emily's room was locked, probably as a precaution against family souvenir hunters. The room was undisturbed and both jewel safes in her closet were firmly shut, but I wasn't interested in them. I pocketed what I needed and left.

I listened for a long time outside Laura's door to be certain that Mrs. Mayfair was gone and that the girl was alone. Water ran and splashed; she was having a long shower to steam away the day's troubles. The water sound cut off and softer, less distinct ones replaced it as she toweled down and padded barefoot around her room.

Her door abruptly opened in my face and her light blue eyes flashed on me in shock and fear. She nearly screamed, but didn't. The house was empty, no one would hear.

She was head to toe in black, her bright blond hair covered by a black scarf.

"Going to a funeral?" I asked.

Her heart jumped and she backed away, but I caught her wrist, swinging her around until she was pressed against the wall. Now she did try to scream, a normal reflex to the situation, but I stopped that with one hand and talked quickly, urgently, focusing in hard enough to crack through her terror. It eventually worked and she relaxed against the wall and I took my hand away from her mouth.

"Where were you going?" I asked.

"The basement."

"Why?"

"I have to get rid of him."

It was no galloping surprise. At this point I was just being thorough. "Did you try to—did you kill Barrett?"

"Yes."

"Why?"

"He knew—knew—" She was struggling against it and could shake it off if she fought hard enough.

"All right, calm down. Everything's okay."

Her breathing smoothed out.

"Go back into your room, lock the door, and sit down."

I followed her in. She chose to sit at her dressing table on a little satin stool much like the one in Bobbi's room. I checked the place, keeping well clear of the veranda windows. The stables were at an oblique angle to them on this side, but there was a chance Haskell might look out and see my figure against her curtains. It was very important that she appear to be alone now.

She was—at least in the mirrors.

It was a cheery place, with yellow flowers blooming in the wallpaper, and a thick rust-colored rug covered most of the floor. The bath was warm and damp from her shower, and that day's black dress was crumpled into a hamper. She'd rinsed her stockings herself and hung them over the shower rod to dry.

I found a chair and dragged it over to face her. In the mirror-covered wall it moved all by itself.

She was very still, waiting for me to speak. Her body rhythms were strong and even. After an active summer of swimming and riding, her skin was tanned and healthy. She was quite a beautiful girl and her youth attracted me even as it must have attracted Barrett.

"Laura, my name is Jack. You remember me from earlier tonight?"

She nodded.

"I'm going to ask you some questions and you will want to answer them. You can tell me the truth, to do so will make you feel very good."

She waited, disinterested and seeing nothing.

"Laura, did you kill Maureen Dumont?"

"Who?"

And that threw me until I realized she might never have heard the name. "Remember the summer of the fire?"

"Yes."

"Remember the dark-haired woman who came one night to see Barrett?"

"Yes."

"Did you kill that woman?"

She'd buried it deep and it didn't want to come out. Her breath got short, and for a second, real awareness came back to her eyes. I steadied her down and soothed her, keeping my voice low, but pitched so she had to listen. I told her it was all right to answer and repeated my question, and then she said yes.

I felt nothing looking into her blank eyes. Her face ceased to belong to a person and took on the smooth, bland beauty of a mannequin. The lost years and the emotional racking and the physical trauma had taken all feeling from me. The worry, fear, and doubt that had once driven me were gone, and I was empty. We mirrored each other now. All I had left were questions, and they weren't really mine, but Escott's.

"Laura, talk to me. Tell me about it. Why did you do it?"

She revealed no surprises. Escott had been right. She was in love with Barrett and had killed to keep him.

"Did you kill Violet that summer?"

"No, the fire did."

It was an odd answer and I picked a subtle change in her tone of voice, as though I were talking to a child. "Did you set the fire in the house?"

"No."

"How did it start?"

"The lamp cord."

"Did you do something to the lamp cord?"

"I fixed it."

"So that it would start the fire?"

"Yes."

"Then you did kill Violet."

"No, the *fire* killed her."

I could argue with her, but to no point. Her exacting logic was how she could live with herself, by shifting the blame. "Why did you kill her?"

For Barrett, all for Barrett. She'd wanted him that badly. She'd frayed the wires and fixed the rug so that air could feed in. All she had to do was turn on the lamp and wait. When the first flames sprang up she went out the door and snuck back to her room.

"How could you do that?"

She gave a little shrug. "It was easy."

Fire and ice inside me and now the same sickness I'd felt when Banks had died.

"How did you kill Maureen?" Someone else seemed to be talking to her but using my voice.

She'd read up about vampires that summer. She knew more about us than Barrett had ever suspected, and she knew what to do.

Being a strong girl, it had been nothing for her to lift Maureen's small body from her trunk to the bath in the bright light of morning. She'd filched a sharp stake of wood from Mayfair's work shed and she had a hammer. Frozen by daylight, Maureen had died without a sound. The only problem for Laura was the blood. Her clothes had been soaked with it and she was frightened she'd be found out. She'd spent hours cleaning it up.

In a cardboard box scavenged from the kitchen she hid Maureen's body. It was very light now, hardly more than a husk. She had no trouble getting it downstairs and out the side door, away from the servants' wing. Dragging it into some trees, she used their cover to take it to the ruins of the old house.

She'd been forbidden to play there, but such rules had never stopped her before. There was a broken spot in the floor above the deepest part of the cellar. It sagged under her weight, but she was careful to move slowly and test each step, pushing the box ahead of her. Grating against the soot and debris, it barely held together. She just managed to get it to the edge and pushed it in.

It had been a rainy summer, but the splash still startled her. She hadn't expected the cellar to be so full of water. A cautious look over the edge showed only a rippling reflection of the sky behind her head. There was no sign of the box or of Maureen's body. She was safe.

The parallels of what happened to Maureen and what nearly happened to me were all too clear in my mind. I knew *exactly* what she had gone through, and inside I was screaming for her. I stood and backed away from Laura. Not all feeling had died. The war was still going on between fiery rage and cold justice. Neither was canceling the other out, both seemed to be fusing together somehow.

"What about Maureen's things?" I asked, a calm stranger once more using my voice.

The only real problem was in getting rid of the woman's

trunk. The earth she mixed in with the flower beds, the clothes Laura took to her room and hid under the bed. She spent the rest of the day reading and dancing by herself before the mirrors, as she usually did.

The household schedule was unorthodox, but regular. The staff did downstairs maintenance until midafternoon, when Emily woke up. After her breakfast, the maid was allowed to work upstairs. No one paid much attention to Laura or her activities. Showing up on time for meals was all that was expected of her.

She and Emily shared supper just before sunset, as usual, then Emily went downstairs to be with Barrett. Whenever Emily was with him, they almost always spent an hour or more together. Laura returned to her own room and changed into Maureen's clothes, called for a cab, and waited by the phone. Both Violet and Emily had been generous concerning her allowance. She had over two hundred dollars on hand. She took it all, not knowing how much it would cost to go to Port Jefferson.

The call came from the gatehouse. Laura answered on the first ring and gave Mayfair permission to let John Henry Banks through. The main danger now was that Barrett might break his pattern because of his guest and come up earlier than usual. He didn't, and she brought the empty trunk safely downstairs and out the front door.

Two minutes later she was on her way to Port Jefferson. Banks dropped her off near the ferry and drove back to Glenbriar to celebrate his five-dollar tip.

"What happened to the trunk?"

"I found stones to put in it and dropped it off the end of a dock."

"You take another cab home?"

"Yes."

She had the Port Jefferson driver drop her near the gate, snuck through, and walked back to the house without being caught. She listened to her radio and danced before her mirror, pretending that Barrett was her partner.

"What did you do with her clothes?"

"I pushed them into the house incinerator. Haskell burned them up the next day with the usual trash."

She watched the trucks and crews roll in and begin tearing down the ruins. The blackened shards of wood were torn away, and the broken glass was removed. What was left of the floor was pounded apart and allowed to cave in to the cellar, which gradually filled with the packed debris. A few days later more trucks came in with topsoil and covered it all like a grave.

All too fitting.

I found it difficult to look at her. "Then you just went on as before?"

"Yes."

"No questions, no guilt?"

She blinked.

"Didn't you feel bad about what you did?"

"Why should I?"

"You killed. You murdered an innocent woman you knew nothing about."

"Well, I *had* to."

No guilt, no regret. A job finished and a goal achieved. Barrett would be hers when the time came.

"What about Barrett? When did he start to notice you as a woman?"

She smiled at the memory. "He's always been looking at me. Always, always, always. I'm young and I'm beautiful and he wants me." The little-girl voice was back again.

"What about Emily?"

"He wants me, not her."

"But what about her?"

"She's dead."

"I know. Did you kill her?"

"I had to."

"Why?"

"She heard us talking."

"About what?"

Barrett had wasted no time last night. After punching me out he went straight home to Laura, finally hypnotizing her to get the truth.

She'd heard about the man asking questions about the fire from the house staff. The story of Banks and his memorable tip came up. She left to find him, to see for herself if he was a danger. She carried along a small suitcase. Inside it was a club.

Parking her car near a gas station with a phone, she called for Banks to come pick her up. They drove a little and she talked with him. Her questions about his Port Jefferson trip clicked things together in his memory, and he recognized her. He thought it to be an amazing coincidence.

She asked him to stop the car and he did so, still chattering about her and how she'd changed. She brought the club out of the suitcase and smashed it into the side of his head as hard as she could. She hit him several times to make sure, then took his money box to make it look like a robbery.

The storm was bad by now, but her car wasn't too far from where they'd stopped. She got out, but before she could get away, another car appeared and she saw the driver talking to Banks. She took care of him as well, then fought her way through the rain to her own vehicle.

Breathless, she tumbled into it and crept home again. She laughed to see a third car in line behind the others as she passed. The frantic man waving at her to stop looked so ridiculous.

Once home, she had the bad luck to be spotted by Barrett. He'd worried that she'd been caught out in the rain and they joked about her wet clothes. Things weren't so funny to him later.

The next night he pressed her for answers and Emily had heard them talking. She didn't know what was going on;

she'd only heard the tone of Barrett's voice, and it frightened her.

"Silly old woman," said Laura. "She should have left me alone. It's all her fault."

"What's her fault?"

"She worried all night and then got up early to talk with me. Jonathan had told me to forget it, but then she started talking, so it's her fault."

"Why did he tell you to forget it?"

"I don't know."

"But you remembered when Emily asked you about it?"

"Yes."

She had only to lie again, to say that Barrett had been scolding her for driving out in the hurricane.

"Then what happened?"

"Then I had to do it again," she said wistfully.

Except for Barrett, Emily had the only other key to his rooms. Laura knew where it was kept and stole it and used it.

Her experience with Maureen left her better prepared to deal with Barrett. This time she stripped to the skin before using her stake and hammer. She cried while she cleaned up, because she did love him.

"I really did, but this was coming and I wish it hadn't happened so soon."

"You planned to kill him anyway?"

"I didn't want to, but he would have spoiled it all."

"Spoiled what?"

"It's Emily's fault, not mine. It's *her* fault he's dead and that I had to take care of her, too. She'd have found out, so I had to take care of her, and it's her fault, not mine, all her fault—"

"Laura, why were you going to kill him before?"

"Because."

She was a complete child now, speaking with a child's voice and using a child's logic. Grown up in so many other ways, something within her was stunted or had never been a part of her at all.

"Laura, tell me why you were going to kill him."

"Because."

"Why?"

"He was going to marry her."

That rocked me back. Now I knew what Barrett had been telling Laura while I'd watched from the window and Bing Crosby sang from the radio. From that night, Barrett had been a doomed man.

"Were you jealous?"

"He was going to get what belonged to me. He was going to have me, but I wasn't enough and he'd get all of it when she died. He'd take it all away because she'd give it to him."

I'd been right; she'd made an investment for her future. She loved Barrett, maybe, but he was nothing compared to Emily's money.

"He should have said no, like all the other times—"

"You mean Emily proposed to him?"

"He should have said no, but this time he said yes and it's *her* fault, not *mine*—"

"Hush, now. It's all right, hush."

She trailed off, her face red with anger, the anger she'd hidden from him so well when he'd told her the news.

"Laura, how do you feel about murder?"

I had to repeat the question. She shook her head.

"Don't you feel anything at all about killing those people?"

Puzzlement. Another head shake.

"How do you think they felt?"

Her face was blank.

"Don't you think they had a right to live?"

She shrugged. It was like explaining light and color to the totally blind. She would never, ever be able to see.

"Are you thirsty, Laura?"

"A little."

"I'll get you a glass of water. Wait right here."

In her bathroom I mixed the stuff with the whiskey and stirred it around in a glass with my finger until it dissolved. I wiped everything clean and took the glass in wrapped in a washcloth. I told her it was cold water and that she was to drink it all.

"Will you write something for me, Laura?"

"Yes."

"Good."

She put down the empty glass and smeared dark pink lip color onto her dressing-table mirror, and I gave her the washcloth to wipe her finger on. The few words scribbled over the glass were for others to read and interpret. For her, they were utterly meaningless.

"You're tired, Laura. It's been a busy day. Go to bed now."

She stretched but didn't yawn, and immediately stripped off her clothes and tucked them neatly into the hamper. She'd dressed for darkness on her way to dispose of Barrett's body, but that task was forgotten as she got ready for a good night's sleep.

I looked under the bed and found the suitcase with his clothes. He was meant to disappear like Maureen. None of the Franchers would be sorry that the fortune hunter had left. No doubt his clothes would have gone into the incinerator for Haskell to burn. I put the case out in the hall and relocked the door.

She brushed out her hair, taking her time and staring at her body in the mirror. Her movements were growing slower and more unsteady as the minutes passed. She put on a nightgown but each action had to be thought out, and in between, she'd pause and try to recall what the next was to be.

She got into bed. The lights were on. I turned them off for her, using the cloth again as I had for the door. I left the bedside table lamp on.

Her eyes canted to the radio and her hand twitched. By

now she'd lost muscle control. I turned it on for her, it warmed up, and we listened to soft dance music.

She was deeply asleep now. Her breathing was slow and shallow even as her pulse speeded up. A thin sheen of sweat appeared on her serene face.

Instead of the sleeping mannequin on the bed, I saw Emily Francher.

I saw John Henry Banks.

I saw a last ghostly image of Maureen flash over my inner eye and spin away forever into memory.

I waited and watched and felt nothing.

Nothing until the time finally came and the room was silent but for the radio.

Nothing until I looked at the scrawl on the mirror and read the words I'd dictated: *I'm sorry. God forgive me.*

Then I bowed my head and tried not to weep.

"How is he?" I asked.

Escott came in and sat across from me. I was in the red leather chair by the cold fireplace staring at the unswept ashes. The candles next to Emily's casket were out, but I'd put on a table lamp so she wouldn't be left in the darkness.

"He's better."

"That's good."

"He was cleaning up and getting dressed when I left him."

My voice sounded a little too normal. "Does he know about Emily?"

"He asked. I only told him she was dead. He did not seem too surprised. I expect he'll be up here before long."

"Did you talk about Laura?"

"Yes. He knew it had been her today."

"I thought he would. What'll he do?"

"I don't know."

We left it at that for a time and listened to the silence of the massive house around us. I'd long since shut off Laura's radio.

I got to my feet. "I'll go find out."

His face was very sad but he said nothing, and I was grateful for that.

I could have walked right through Barrett's door, but knocked and waited instead. After a long minute he said to come in and I did, leaving the suitcase with his clothes by the bed.

He was in his library seated on a long couch. He'd pulled on some pants and slippers, but his shirt was buttoned only halfway, as though he'd forgotten to finish the job. There was a new weariness in his expression, the kind that comes from a tired soul and not just a tired body. His arms hugged his chest, a gesture I could commiserate with; I'd felt the same when it had happened to me.

I stood in the doorway, hands jammed in my pockets. "Glad you're better."

He nodded. "Your friend didn't seem to want to hear it, so I'll say it to you: thank you for pulling me back."

I shrugged self-consciously, beginning to understand Escott's attitude. "He's the one who got me moving. Haskell helped a lot, too."

"Haskell? Did you influence him?"

"At first, but he woke out of it. He kept going, though. He knows about you."

"Well, well."

"Says he'd seen you with the horses."

"And he accepts me anyway. I'll be thanking him, too."

"Yeah."

He mused for a while and looked up, afraid to hope. "Is there any change in Emily?"

"Not the last I saw her. How long did it take for Maureen?"

" 'Twas on the same night she died."

"Same for me. For what it's worth, I'm sorry all this happened."

He accepted, numbly. "Thank you." He gestured at a chair. I declined and remained in the doorway.

"I need to talk to you about Laura."

He shook his head. "No, you don't, Mr. Fleming. Not one word. I've been a fool's fool over that girl and there's no excuse for me. You were both right. I wish to God I'd realized it earlier—"

"She . . . she pushed Emily."

He faltered.

"She remembered you questioning her; that's why she came here to kill you. Then she had to kill Emily to cover up your death."

The pain rolled off him like a tidal wave and I stayed there and let it hit me. I said nothing about the money or anything stupid like that because the man was falling apart in front of me, and I stared at the floor for the whole time and pretended not to see or hear him.

Later he mumbled something about talking to Laura.

"No, Barrett, stay here."

"I have to—"

"She's dead."

The man was in pieces already and it was my lot to smash them into smaller shards.

"I found her. She'd put some sleeping pills in a drink."

The truth, but not all of it. He didn't want to believe it and then he couldn't help but believe it. All he had to do was look up at my face and see it there. I stared at the damned floor and memorized the carpet pattern.

"I think maybe it was too much for her, and in the end she was sorry." The one thing I could give him was the cold comfort of a lie. He needed it badly.

Then it came pouring out of him, and I listened and let him talk because he had to get it all out. He repeated what I'd learned from Laura, everything about Violet and Maureen and Banks; the words tumbling swiftly until they ceased to be words and turned into an unintelligible drone.

"I wish I could have helped her," he said at the end.

"You could have," I said, adding one more lie to give substance to his illusion.

He accepted it.

Escott was cooling his heels in the main hall outside the parlor when I came up.

"Ready to go home?" I asked.

"What about Barrett?"

"We talked. He'll be all right."

"What will he do?"

"I don't know, but he'll be all right."

"Did you tell him about Laura?"

"He knows she's dead." Barrett didn't need or want the truth. Maybe he'd figure it out someday, but he didn't need it now.

Barrett walked up. His shoulders drooped, but he'd buttoned his shirt and tucked it in. It was a minor thing, but I took it as a good sign.

"I thought I'd ride with you as far as the gate," he said. "The Mayfairs will be long asleep by now and I'd rather not disturb them."

I started to say something, but forgot it—a small, soft sound distracted me. Barrett heard it, too, and automatically swiveled his head in the right direction. From where I stood I could see the parlor and noticed a white rose lying on the floor next to the casket. It was the rose Emily held to her breast. Somehow it had fallen out.

Barrett stared at us with sudden, agonized hope and dashed in to her.